Gideon's Ghost

—

Gregory Stout

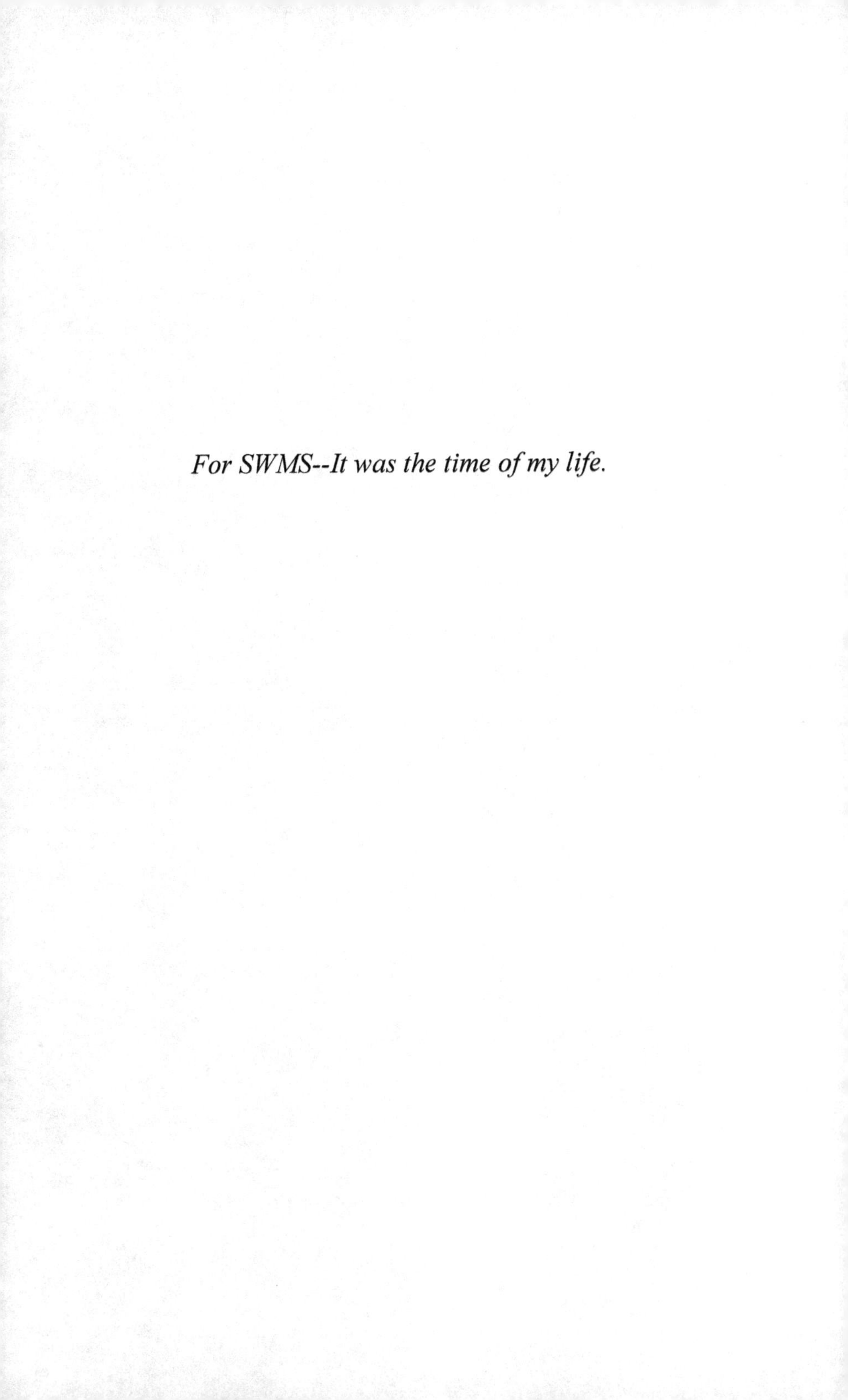

For SWMS--It was the time of my life.

CHAPTER ONE:

A Terrible Accident

On the first Tuesday in June 1965 at ten o'clock in the morning, my father stopped at a tavern on the way back to his office after meeting with a customer. Two hours later he crashed his car head-on into a telephone pole. When the police arrived, they found him unconscious and bleeding from a massive head injury. He was taken by ambulance to a St. Louis hospital. Within minutes after he arrived in the emergency room a priest was summoned to administer the last sacraments of the Roman Catholic Church.

*   *   *   *

"Your father has had an accident. He has been hurt very badly."

I sat at the kitchen table that night with my mother as she tried to explain the terrible thing that had happened.

"The doctor says he's got injuries on the inside of his head. There is swelling and pressure on his brain from the bleeding. Right now, he can't talk or move, so we don't know yet if he has suffered any permanent damage." Her voice was strained, and her eyes were red from crying. "For now, all we can do is pray and wait to hear from the hospital."

I said, "Is he going to die?"

"No, honey, he's not," Mom said. "Your dad is a young man and he's got a lot of fight in him. It's going to take some time. He'll be fine, but right now it looks like he could be in the hospital for quite a while. That means—how do I say this? That means without your father around things are going to have to be a little different here at home until he gets better."

Mom looked me in the eye when she said it, but I could tell there was something more she wasn't telling me. I wanted to ask what "quite a while" meant. More than that, I wanted to ask what "a little different" meant. But what I asked instead was, "When can I see him?"

"I don't know if that's a good idea just now, Gary. It might be better if you waited until he's feeling a little better. Right now he doesn't look very good and he isn't going to be able to speak to you at all."

"I don't care," I said, sticking my chin out. "I want to see him."

"I know you do, and I understand, but you have to trust me, this is not a good time."

"Then when?"

"Can we talk about it in the morning?" she asked. "Please? I'm really tired. I've been at the hospital since two-thirty this afternoon. I've got to make some phone calls and I need time to work a few things out."

She came around to the other side of the table where I was sitting and hugged me. Then she went into her bedroom and closed the door. After a few minutes I heard her talking on the telephone. I couldn't make out through the door the exact words she was saying, but I supposed she was calling family and friends to let them know about Dad.

The last call went on longer than the others, and partway through she raised her voice and I could hear her say, "Well, damn it, Sophie, what else can I do?" I knew then that she was talking to my Grandmother Seiler, Dad's mother. I heard her say, "No, it has to be Friday." After that her voice got quiet, and a few minutes later she hung up the phone. Then the light spilling out from under her door went dark and the only sound I could hear was my mother crying.

I went into my own room, closed the door and got undressed for bed, and even though it was close to midnight, sleep would not come. I tried to organize the questions swirling around in my head into a list that made sense, but the harder I tried the more tangled things got until I no longer knew where to start. And although I had a lot more questions for Mom, there was one I didn't need to ask, and that was how Dad managed to run into a telephone pole in broad daylight driving a car that was barely a year old. I didn't need to ask because I already knew the answer.

He was drunk again.

CHAPTER TWO:

At the Hospital

After a restless night, I was out of bed early.
Mom was already up, sitting at the kitchen table. A
cup of coffee was on the table in front of her. She
was smoking a cigarette and looking out the
window into the front yard. From the tired look on
her face, I guessed she hadn't slept any better than I
did.

I asked, "Are you going to the hospital
today?"

She nodded. "I'm leaving as soon as I get
dressed."

"I'm coming with you."

"Oh, Gary, I thought we talked about that.
I'm going to be there all day and you won't have a
way to get home. And besides, you've got school."

I had already guessed that's what she would say and had my answer ready. "This is the last week before vacation. Nobody is going to miss me for one day. I'll just stay long enough to see how he is and then I can take the bus home."

I thought we were heading for an argument, but then she sighed and nodded. "Okay, you can come. I need to discuss something with you anyway. I was going to save it for tonight, but we can talk in the car." She stubbed out her cigarette and emptied what was left of her coffee into the sink. "Let me just call school and let them know you'll be staying home today."

Half an hour later we were in the car, heading into the city. I waited for mom to tell me what it was she wanted to talk to me about, but after almost twenty minutes she still hadn't said anything. She was caught up in her own thoughts, and I was trying to figure out a good way to say what I wanted to say. Finally, I decided there might never be a better chance than right now and that I should just go ahead and say what I was thinking.

"He was drunk again, wasn't he? That's how he wrecked the car, right? I mean it was the middle of the day, it wasn't raining, and phone poles don't just jump off the side of the road in front of you."

"I don't know. It looks that way, but he's also been taking a new medication for his blood pressure, so that might have had something to do with it. I'm hoping we'll find out something more when we see Dr. Oswald today."

"Was he arrested? Did he get a DUI?" I remembered my friend Phil's older brother was banged up in a car crash one time and wound up getting arrested for drunk driving after the ambulance had taken him to the emergency room at the hospital.

"Well, technically, he's in custody, but obviously he wasn't taken to the police station. I'm not sure what happens next."

That is some technicality, I thought, arresting a man who is unconscious. Wonder if they cuffed him.

We drove the last few blocks without further conversation. Mom pulled into the visitor parking lot and turned off the engine.

"Are you sure you want to do this?" she asked me. "He doesn't look very good, and I don't need you freaking out in the middle of the ICU."

"I'm not going to freak out," I said, though now that we were actually at the hospital my imagination was kicking into high gear and I wondered whether coming along had been the right decision after all.

We walked through the reception area and rode the elevator up to a floor marked INTENSIVE CARE. When the elevator doors opened we were hit with a smell that was somewhere between laundry detergent and rubbing alcohol. The intensive care unit was cool, brightly lit and very quiet.

Directly in front of the elevator door was a nurses' station with a sign that read, "Please register with receptionist." Another sign in bigger letters said OXYGEN IN USE. Below that it said POSITIVELY NO SMOKING.

"Wait here." Mom stopped at the nurses' station to speak to a woman wearing a white uniform and cap. She said something to the nurse and then nodded her head a couple of times. After that she motioned for me to follow her.

I don't know what I expected to see. I knew he'd suffered a head injury, so I guessed he would have a bandage on his head. Other than that, I imagined he'd look more or less okay, like maybe he was just taking a nap.

My father did not look anything close to okay. In fact, at first, I thought we must have been in the wrong room and this was some other man I had never seen before. He was lying in the bed with his eyes open. His chest rose and fell in time with a respirator that was doing his breathing for him, and his eyes would blink occasionally. Those were the only indications that he was even alive. With all of the tubes and wires connected to his motionless body he looked like a man trapped in a web spun by some fantastic spider.

There was a tube that ran from the respirator into his mouth. Wide strips of white tape held the tube in place. A second, smaller tube had been inserted into his nose. Another was attached to a needle sticking into his arm. Wire leads connected him to a heart monitor and a cuff on his left arm was connected to a device that measured his blood pressure. The most frightening thing, however, was not the machinery; it was my father himself, looking as he did like the subject of an experiment in a horror movie. The hair on the left side of his scalp had been shaved away and a hole had been drilled into the side of his head. There was a tube sticking out just over his ear with a bandage holding it in place. The tube was filled with pinkish fluid that was dripping slowly into a jar hanging from a stand next to his bed. One end of the bed was elevated so that he was sitting up a little.

I stood there with my mouth open struggling with the realization that the man in the bed was my father. My knees started to get wobbly and it felt like the floor was moving beneath my feet.

I said, "Dad?"

No answer.

I called his name again, thinking he might at least turn his head to look at me, but he didn't respond. Not even his eyes moved. They just kept looking at a spot on the wall.

Mom had been right. Coming here was a bad idea. A very bad idea.

Mom said, "I don't know if he can understand you, Gary. Maybe he can, or maybe he knows we're here, but he can't respond just yet." Then, guessing my next question, she added, "The tube in his head is to relieve pressure from the bleeding. We're not sure how long that will have to stay in, but there's fluid accumulating inside his head and that has to be drained away. The one in his mouth is to help him breathe and to keep his lungs clear, so he doesn't get pneumonia. The needle in his arm is for medication. The one in his nose is for oxygen. The others are because, well, he can't get up and go to the bathroom."

There was a noise in my ear like a telephone ringing. A voice that sounded like someone else's asked, "Will he get better?"

"I hope so, honey. I'm sure praying for him."

"How can he eat with all that stuff in his mouth?"

"He can't. Right now, they're just giving him fluids to keep him from dehydrating."

The ringing noise in my ears was getting more insistent, and I knew I needed to get out of that room. I turned to leave, and as I did I ran headlong into a man coming through the doorway.

"Excuse me," I said, then stepped back to see who I had bumped into. He was tall, wearing a white shirt with a blue necktie and a white lab coat. A pair of glasses was propped up on top of his head. He was carrying a clipboard. And to my surprise, he was a colored man.

My mother said, "Gary, this is Dr. Oswald. Doctor, this is my son, Gary."

"Pleased to meet you, Gary," the doctor said, and held out his hand. I hesitated a moment before shaking it.

My mother asked, "Any change since yesterday?"

"I'm afraid not," said Dr. Oswald. He had a very deep voice, and when he spoke he pronounced every syllable of every word very clearly. "As you can see, the fluid that is draining from his head is still not clear, so that means there is still bleeding. We did an X-ray earlier this morning, but as I explained last night, until we get the bleeding under control we can't really get a clear enough look at what's going on to determine whether any damage has been done to the brain itself.

"Here," he said, "let me just take a quick look."

I watched the doctor as he examined my father. He shined a light in his eyes, moving it from side to side. I might have missed it, but it didn't look like his eyes were following the light. He tapped the inside of Dad's elbow with a small hammer, and Dad's arm twitched reflexively. He checked the machines at Dad's bedside, noting his heart and respiration rate. He lifted a corner of Dad's blanket and tickled the bottom of his foot with the tip of his pen. There was no response.

"Okay, Mrs. Seiler," he said to Mom as he wrote something on his clipboard. "Maybe we could step outside for a minute." Then he turned to me. "Gary, I want to talk to your mom and then I need to look in on some other patients, but before I go are there any questions I can answer for you?"

"I don't know, I don't think so," I said. At that moment I was having trouble gathering my thoughts. I don't think I could have told him what city we were in.

He looked at me and smiled. "I'll bet I can guess what's on your mind."

"You can?" I said, suddenly terrified that he really did know and that he was going to say it out loud for Mom to hear.

"Yes. You're worried that your dad might not get better and you're wondering if we're going to be able to get him well again. Am I right?"

I nodded yes, grateful that he didn't say what he knew I was thinking.

"Gary, this is the best hospital from here to Chicago for treating head injuries like your dad has. Believe me; we'll take care of him for you."

"Promise you'll get him well again?" I asked.

"I can't say that for sure, but I can promise we'll do the best we can," he said. "How soon he gets better is really more up to him than it is to us, okay?" He offered me his hand again, and this time I took it without hesitation.

CHAPTER THREE:

A Voice in the Dark

It was past noon when Mom and I took the elevator down to the hospital cafeteria for lunch. She ordered a chicken salad sandwich and a cup of coffee. After the experience I had just had, my stomach was rolling over and I wasn't feeling very hungry. But neither of us had eaten any breakfast, and Mom said we should have something, so I ordered a bowl of chili and a Coke.

"What did the doctor tell you after you left the room?" I asked.

"Nothing very definite, I'm afraid, except that it's only been twenty-four hours or so and we shouldn't get discouraged."

"That was all? It took him ten minutes to tell you that?"

She picked up her sandwich and then put it down again without eating any of it. "No, there was more. He said that if there is going to be any improvement we should start to see something within about two weeks."

"What happens if we don't? What then?"

"Why don't we worry about that when the time comes, okay? We have enough to think about right now without getting panicky about things that might never happen."

My next question made me uneasy, but I asked it anyway. "Mom, since when have there been colored doctors?"

"There have always been colored doctors, Gary. You've just never been to one because we don't live in the same part of town as colored people. Look," she said, leaning across the table toward me, "I know what you're thinking, but times are changing. Laws are changing. I spoke with one of the nurses here last night and she told me Doctor Oswald is the best neurologist they've got. Frankly, if he can help your father, I don't care if he's green."

I could feel my face starting to burn. "I just

meant...."

She reached across the table and covered my hand with hers. "I know what you meant," she said gently. "Find something else to worry about. Doctor Oswald is the best thing your dad has got going for him right now."

Feeling worse by the minute, I ate only a little of my chili, which was getting cold and didn't taste very good anyway. "I better get going," I said. "I need to get over to the park, so I can catch my bus."

Mom nodded. "Before you go, I have to tell you something else. I was going to mention it in the car, but I didn't want you to get upset before we went up to see your father. I talked to your grandmother Seiler down in Fairweather last night. I had to call and let her know what happened."

"I understand," I said.

"No, you don't," Mom said, "I talked to her for quite a while, and obviously she's as worried as we are. She offered to come up and help out for a while, but I convinced her there wasn't anything she could really do, and I didn't need extra people in the house. So, and I know you're not going to like this, she agreed instead to let you come down to Fairweather and spend a few weeks with her and Granddad and your Uncle Bob, at least until we know for sure how long it will be before we can get your dad back on his feet and out of the hospital."

"Wait a minute, what? You're sending me to Oklahoma for the summer?" Up to that point I would have said it was impossible for things to be any worse than they already were, but this news was like getting hit with a brick. I said, "No way, you can't do this! I'm staying right here. It isn't my fault this happened!"

"Of course, it's not your fault. Nobody said it was."

"Then why am I the one getting screwed?"

"Watch your language," she said. "You're not getting screwed; you're going to visit your grandparents for a little while."

"I don't want to visit them. Vacation starts next week, and I've got stuff to do this summer. I don't want to waste the whole three months with Grandmother and Granddad."

"It's not going to be three months. Once Dad starts showing some improvement, you can come back."

"And if he doesn't, does that mean I have to live there for the rest of my life?"

"That kind of talk isn't helping at all, Gary. You know better than that."

"Besides, Grandmother Seiler doesn't like us. You said so yourself."

"She likes you fine, Gary. It's me she doesn't care much for. You won't have any problem with her at all."

"I don't care," I said, my voice rising in anger. "Just because Dad is a drunk who can't drive in a straight line is no reason why I should have to waste my summer in some crap town in Oklahoma where I don't know anybody and there's nothing to do."

"Keep your voice down!" Mom said sharply. Then, in a milder tone she said, "Gary, I know you're upset, and I know today has been hard for you, but you need to listen to me. Until your dad gets better I'm going to have a lot of extra work to do. I have to be here at the hospital every day. I have to go to work. I have to pay the bills, take care of the house, and much as I hate to say it, I'm just not going to have a lot of time left to be worrying about you."

"I can take care of myself. You said so yourself lots of times. I can cook and do laundry. I'll be just fine by myself." That was a weak argument and I knew it, but I could see my summer vacation slipping away.

She shook her head. "You can make toast, open cans and warm up leftovers. After that, you're more likely to set the kitchen on fire than fix anything you can actually eat."

I started to say something else, but she cut me off with a wave.

"Gary, I'm not going to argue with you. I love your father and he needs me for as much of the time as I can possibly give him. I love you, too, more than you can imagine, but right now I simply can't do everything. I realize this is not how you wanted to spend your summer, but it's not what Dad or I wanted either. If you really want to help me, just do what I ask."

"But Mom...."

"No, we're done here. When I talked to your principal this morning I let her know tomorrow will be your last day. There's only another week of school left before vacation, and she assured me your grades are fine and that it's okay for you to miss the rest of the year. I also got you a train ticket for Friday morning, so tonight and tomorrow night we'll have to wash clothes and get you packed."

I tried one last time. "But I was going to work on my golf game this summer. You know I was going to try out for the team this fall."

"They have golf courses in Fairweather," she said, and her tone of voice made it clear that was the end of the discussion.

*　　　　　　*　　　　　　*　　　　　　*

The bus ride home took me past the golf course in Forest Park where I play two or three times a week during the summer and on Saturdays in the fall until cold weather set in. Most of the time I play with my best friend Phil, who is the same age as me and who uses a hand-me-down set of clubs his dad bought for himself when he was thinking about taking up the game and then never did.

I started golfing when I was eleven, and here's the thing: I like sports, but I'm terrible at everything I've ever tried to play except golf. I can't hit a curve ball, can't break a dinner plate with my fastball and every ground ball hit my way winds up going through my legs into the outfield. I'm not big enough or fast enough for football and I couldn't shoot a basket if the hoop were the size of a manhole. For some reason, though, I have no problem hitting a ball that's not moving. I earned the money to buy my first set of clubs caddying at a country club near our house. That summer I met a couple other caddies who liked to play and pretty soon we were out hitting the ball every Friday morning when the course was closed for maintenance and the groundskeeper would turn the caddies loose on the holes they had finished mowing. Turned out, I have a talent for it, because by the end of the first summer I was breaking an honest hundred. Three years later, and after saving up to pay for a couple lessons from the club pro, I was shooting in the high 80s, so that on a good day I can beat about sixty percent of everybody who plays, at least if they actually play by the rules and count all their strokes. My junior high school didn't have a golf team, but the high school I would be attending in the fall did. I felt pretty confident that if I could keep practicing during the summer, when tryouts started in August, I'd have a good chance to make the team. Now it looked like that might have to wait for another year.

When I got home I called Phil to tell him about Dad and that it looked like I was going to be gone for at least part of the summer.

"I heard about your dad at school," he told me. "That really sucks. Did you find out what happened? Nobody at school knew anything except he passed out in his car and had an accident. Did he have a heart attack or something?"

"They don't know yet. It might have been something wrong with the car." That was a lie, of course, the same kind of lie Mom and I had been telling people every time my father was "too sick" to attend a school event or a family birthday, or when he was "out of town visiting relatives" when he was actually in the hospital drying out from having consumed too much alcohol. And even though Mom and I did our best to cover up the truth, I'm pretty sure everybody who knew us knew what was going on.

"Did the doctor say how long before he gets out of the hospital?"

"He didn't say anything about that to me, but the way he was talking to Mom, I think it might be more like 'if'."

"So how long do you think you might have to stay with your grandmother?"

"I don't know. If he gets better right away, maybe I'll just be there a couple of weeks. I hope that's it."

In the background I heard Phil's mom say, "Tell Gary we're awfully sorry about his dad. Tell him to ask his mother if there's anything we can do."

Phil said, "My mom said," but I cut him off.

"I heard. Tell her thanks and I'll let my mom know."

There was a pause. "How are you going to get down there?"

"I'm going down on the train. Dad works for the Frisco Railroad, remember?"

Phil started to ask me something else, but I said, "I've got to go. Mom wants me to pack a bunch of stuff tonight and I haven't even started. I'll see you tomorrow at school, okay?"

Right after I hung up with Phil, Mom called and said she was waiting to talk to the doctor before he left for the day and that she would be staying late at the hospital, so I was on my own for dinner. I looked around in the refrigerator and found some left over meat loaf. I couldn't find any gravy to warm it up with, so I cut a couple of slices and made a cold meat loaf sandwich with potato chips.

While I was cleaning up the phone rang. I picked up, hoping it was Mom again, this time with some good news, but it was a neighbor asking about Dad and offering to bring over some supper for Mom and me. I told her thanks, Mom was still at the hospital and I'd already eaten, but I'd tell Mom she called. I didn't know what to do after that, so I watched television for a while and then I went outside and sat down on the back-porch swing. I listened to the crickets and tried to let my mind go blank, but no matter how hard I tried, I could not erase from my mind the events of the day or the image of my father lying helplessly in a hospital bed.

It was starting to get dark, and after a while, I sort of drifted off. I don't know how long I was asleep, or if I was dreaming, but suddenly I was startled awake by a familiar voice coming from somewhere close by.

Very clearly the voice said, "Gary, you have nothing to be afraid of. Everything is going to be all right. I'll be seeing you very soon." But when I looked around in the fading light to see who had been talking, there wasn't another soul in sight.

CHAPTER FOUR:

Vacation Begins

The next day at school—my last day at
Thomas Hart Benton Junior High School—went by
in a total blur. I went from one class to the next,
turning in books and sitting through reviews for
final exams that I wasn't going to be around to take.
In the hallway between classes kids kept coming up
to me asking how Dad was doing and telling me
how sorry they were. Even Wallace Warner, who
looks like he's about twenty-two years old and still
in the eighth grade stopped me in the hall to say,
"Too bad about your old man, Seiler. Hope he gets
better."

I gave him a cautious look, expecting his next words to be a wisecrack, or else a demand for my lunch money, but his expression was sincere.

"Thanks," I said. "I hope so, too."

When I got to the cafeteria at lunch period I found Phil waiting at the table where we usually sat. It was the first chance we'd had to talk since last night. We've been best friends since first grade, but this year we haven't seen each other much during the school day because except for lunch and first period home room our schedules are completely different. I debated telling him about the voice I had heard the night before telling me that things would be all right, but then, just as I had with Mom, I decided not to. As it was, I wasn't really sure whether what I heard was real, or just something I dreamed.

"So," he asked me, "how's your day going, or should I not ask?"

"Okay, I guess. A lot of people have told me they feel bad for me and wished me luck and stuff. I appreciate it, but all it's doing is making me feel worse."

"They're just trying to be nice. They don't know what else to say. Heck, I don't know what else to say."

"I know, but just the same." I stared at the food on my tray. Thursday is hamburger day, and most times I eat two, but now that I was only a day away from being put on a train to Oklahoma I wasn't feeling very hungry. I took a couple of bites from one and let the other sit on my plate untouched. This did not escape Phil's notice.

"Are you going to eat that other one?"

"No, take it."

"Okay, if you're sure," he said, and proceeded to snatch it off my tray. "You know, you're going to miss my speech at the graduation ceremony. It's going to be a great moment in Benton history."

I did know. Phil was the smartest kid in the entire school. He had carried a straight-A average all three years and had been chosen to give the valedictory speech at graduation.

"Did Wendy say anything to you?" Wendy is Phil's cousin. She's the same age as Phil and me and she rides the same bus as he does, which is not the bus I ride. Wendy and I are not in any classes together, and because she's in band, our lunch periods are not the same, either.

I've had a pretty major thing for Wendy all year, and I'm pretty sure she likes me too, but so far nothing much has come of it except "hellos" in the hallway and a few chance meetings at the mall or the park. It's gotten so I can't count all the times I've started to call her on the phone to talk or ask her to go to a movie only to lose my nerve and hang up halfway through dialing her number. If only calling up a girl was as easy as hitting a golf ball.

"She said to tell you that she was sorry to hear about your dad. Also, if you wanted to talk, you should give her a call."

"Wait, what? She actually said that?"

"Yeah, of course she did, what's the matter with you? She likes you, don't you know that? She's always asking me why you don't ever talk to her."

I wanted to reach across the table and shake him. "And you never thought to tell me that because?"

"She told me not to. She said she supposed you'd figure it out for yourself when you were ready."

A million other questions, all about Wendy, popped into my head, but the bell rang before I had a chance to ask them. Three more periods to go and then my junior high school career would be over.

At the end of the day I was called down to the principal's office. Mrs. Sorensen told me how sorry she was about Dad and wished me the best of luck next fall when I started high school. She even came around her desk and hugged me. Then said come back and see us when you can, and just like that, my time at Thomas Hart Benton came to an end.

That afternoon Mom called to tell me she was staying late at the hospital again. "I bought some TV dinners and stuck them in the freezer. There's fried chicken and baked turkey, I think. Just put one in the oven and follow the directions on the package. I'm sorry I don't have anything better, but it was the quickest thing I could come up with."

"Don't worry about it," I told her. "I'll be fine. How's Dad? Did you talk to the doctor?"

There was a short silence. "Doctor says he's about the same. If nothing changes in the next few days they're going to bring in a therapist to exercise him every day so that when he wakes up he won't have so much trouble getting his movement back."

"Don't you mean if he wakes up?" I said, and immediately regretted it.

"Gary…."

"Never mind, I'm sorry. I didn't mean that. I'll talk to you later."

I hung up the phone and went into the kitchen to get dinner started. It was just after five o'clock, and according to the directions on the package it was going to take forty-five minutes to cook the frozen dinner. Add fifteen minutes for the oven to warm up and I figured I'd be eating by six. I debated whether to call Wendy now, or wait until after dinner. Since I didn't know what time supper was at her house, I decided to wait until later when I figured she'd have more time to talk. Of course, I didn't have the first idea what I was going to say to her, so I also needed some time to think of something.

"Hi, Wendy, I guess you heard about my dad..."

"Hi, Wendy, Phil said you wanted me to give you a call..."

"Oh, hi, Wendy, guess where I'm spending the summer..."

Crap, there was no way I was going to be able to do this. I put a turkey dinner in the oven and while it was heating up tried to think of something I could talk about with Wendy that wouldn't make me sound like the idiot she obviously already thought I was.

An hour later I was camped out in the living room, eating dinner and watching television. This was a first for me, eating a meal with the TV on. Dad always made sure that no matter what else was going on, we would all sit down as a family and eat our evening meal together. Sometimes we talked about what happened at school that day, or something from Dad's work. Now and then Mom and Dad talked about people I didn't know or something taking place in the news, and other times it seemed like nobody had anything to say and then we'd just sit and eat without much conversation. But we never watched television or took a telephone call during mealtime. That was the rule.

At six o'clock at night there wasn't anything on TV except the news on all four channels. The big story, as it had been for many months, was the war in Vietnam. President Johnson said things were going pretty well for our army, but that we might need to send more troops before the end of the summer. I hoped they were right about the war going well. Some of my friends had older brothers serving in Vietnam. Their parents don't say too much about it except that they're proud of them and hope they'll be coming home soon. I hoped so, too. Dad says the President believes it's important to stop Communism from spreading all over the world, and if we have to fight this war to do it, it's just the price we pay to live in a free country. Personally, I don't see how a little country like Vietnam could be much of a threat to the United States, but Dad says that's because I'm not looking at the bigger picture, whatever that is.

After I ate, I washed my knife and fork, and took out the trash before heading back to the living room to watch more TV. I spent another hour finishing my packing, and then finally got up the nerve to call Wendy.

Wendy's mom answered. "She's not here right now," her mom told me. "She's at her girlfriend's house studying for her science final. Her father's going to pick her up about nine-thirty, but I think that might be a little late to call back." There was a pause, then, "Is this Gary?"

"Yes, ma'am," I said.

"Oh, Gary, we're all so sorry to hear about your father. Is he doing any better?"

"Not yet. Mom is at the hospital now, but so far there hasn't been any change."

"Well, you tell your mother if there's anything we can do she should just let us know, okay?"

"Thanks, I will."

"I'll let Wendy know you called. I'm sure she'll see you at school tomorrow."

Actually, she won't, I wanted to tell her. *She won't see me tomorrow or any other day any time soon because I'll be stuck three hundred and fifty miles from here for who knows how long with my grandparents and my seventeen-year old Uncle Bob who I barely know. My whole summer is shot to hell and I won't see my friends, and this fall I won't make the golf team and none of this is fair and I'm so mad I want to scream at the whole world.*

That's what I wanted to say. But instead, I said, "Thanks very much. I'll see her tomorrow." And I hung up.

CHAPTER FIVE:
The Will Rogers

Friday morning, I was standing with Mom on the platform of the Frisco Railroad depot in Webster Groves. Piled next to me were two suitcases, a duffel bag and my golf clubs. We were waiting for the 8:55 train, the *Will Rogers*, which ran between St. Louis and Oklahoma City. My ticket was for Afton, Oklahoma, the closest stop to Fairweather, the town where my grandparents lived.

"Grandmother and Granddad will pick you up at the station. Your train gets in about five-thirty, so they should be there waiting. Do you remember what they look like?"

I remembered all right, and anyone who has ever read the nursery rhyme "Jack Sprat could eat no fat, his wife could eat no lean," would know what they looked like, too. Grandmother, as she insisted on being called, was a very large woman. She was tall, wide and loud and stomped around her house like a hunter trying to scare up game. And although I could remember hearing her laugh, I couldn't remember ever seeing her smile. Grandmother kept her wiry gray hair pulled into a tight bun at the back of her head. Her face was plain and flat, and except for a pair of diamond earrings, she seemed perfectly content to leave it that way.

Granddad, as Grandmother preferred that he be called, was as opposite from Grandmother as he could be. Granddad was a short, slender man with black hair that he kept neatly trimmed, and dark brown eyes. The story I had heard from Mom was that he was part Cherokee Indian, although Granddad had never said as much himself. Unlike Grandmother, Granddad always seemed to be smiling, as if he knew something really cool that

nobody else had heard about yet. He smoked a pipe
that he always had trouble keeping lit. Granddad
worked for Railway Express, which is a company
that ships small packages on passenger trains. He
didn't drive anything but a tractor, so Grandmother
or my Uncle Bob took him to work every morning
and picked him up every night. He didn't talk much,
but then, living with Grandmother, he didn't have
to. She did enough talking for the both of them and
Uncle Bob besides.

In the distance, I heard a train horn. The
baggage man came out of the depot and put my
duffel bag, my golf clubs and the bigger of my two
suitcases on a cart, then rolled it down to the far end
of the platform. In another minute, the train was
pulling in: two red diesels trimmed in yellow
followed by about a dozen dark green mail and
express cars and a couple of red and silver coaches.

"Now there isn't a diner on this train," Mom
told me as I got settled into my seat. "But there's a
twenty-minute stop at Newburg so you'll be able to
get something to eat at the station there. They have

a lunch counter. Here's fifty dollars." She handed me an envelope with five ten dollar bills inside. "That should keep you for a couple of weeks. There're also some stamps in there so you can write once in a while." She looked at me, hard. "I expect to hear from you."

"What, they don't have a phone?"

"Long distance is expensive. A stamp costs a nickel. It won't kill you to write a letter."

"Okay."

"Not good enough. Promise me you'll write."

"I'll write. I promise," I said.

"Okay, now I've got to go. Give me a kiss." I did, and she turned to go. Through the window, I saw the conductor help my mother down off the train. She stopped to talk to him for a moment, and I could see him nod his head. He had a sympathetic look on his face, and I guessed that either he had heard about Dad from somebody at the railroad, or else my mother had just told him. He turned and looked toward where I was sitting and nodded again. Then he threw the step box into the vestibule and climbed aboard. I heard the door at the end of the car bang shut; there were two short horn blasts from the locomotives and the train began to pull away. My mother was standing on the platform, waving. I waved back until she was out of sight.

The train ride through Missouri was a big nothing. For part of the way the track ran alongside Highway 66, and I kept myself entertained by watching the cars and trucks that all seemed to be going faster than we were. Occasionally I heard the horn from the locomotives and then we would roll past a highway crossing. Sometimes people waved to the train, and I noticed a few of the other passengers waving back. Once I saw a long freight train headed by four black and yellow freight locomotives waiting in a siding for the *Will Rogers* to pass.

Just after eleven o'clock the train stopped in a town called Rolla. A sign next to the tracks said, "Welcome to Rolla, Home of the Missouri School of Mines." I knew that was an engineering college because Phil's dad had gotten his degree there. We waited while three people got off the train and six more boarded. While we were sitting, I looked out the window on the side opposite the depot. An old man, shabbily dressed and unsteady on his feet, unzipped his pants and began peeing on the side of a building. He didn't seem concerned that anyone aboard the train might see him. Maybe he thought no one was watching, or maybe he just didn't care.

*   *   *   *

It was the summer of 1959 and our family had taken a vacation at the Lake of the Ozarks. Along on the trip were Dad, Mom, me and my mother's Aunt Edna, who was afraid to fly but liked to travel and didn't mind cooking for me, so Mom and Dad could go out to eat a few evenings while we were at the lake.

The place we stayed at wasn't anything fancy; just a cluster of small cabins arranged along a gravel driveway that looped around the property. At one end of the resort was a lodge building that had a dining room, a bar and a patio where people could sit outside and watch the sunset over the lake. Another driveway led down a hill to the lake where there was a boat dock and a swimming beach.

During the day, if we didn't go to the beach, we all got into the car and went to Camdenton or Hurricane Deck to visit souvenir shops. One day we went to a place that advertised a two-headed snake. Mom wasn't interested in that, but Dad said it might be worth seeing, so he paid a dollar each to see it. It was there all right, but it was a gimmick. The snake was dead and preserved in a jar of formaldehyde.

The last night of our vacation Aunt Edna cooked supper at the cabin while Mom and Dad met another couple for dinner at the lodge building. It was late when they got back. Aunt Edna and I were already sleeping, but they made a lot of noise coming in and they woke me up. I could tell from their voices that they had both been drinking, so I just lay quietly until they went to bed.

After a while, things settled down and I fell back asleep. I don't know how much time went by, but I heard a noise and woke up again. It was still

*　　　　*　　　　*　　　　*

About forty minutes after we left Rolla the
train pulled into Newburg. The conductor said we
would be there for twenty minutes while a new
crew boarded to take the train as far as Springfield.
That gave me time to get off and go into the depot
for something to eat. The lunch counter was
crowded and there was no place to sit, so I
wandered back outside where there was a man
selling sandwiches and soda pop off the back of a
truck. The sandwiches looked like they'd been there

a while, so I got a couple of bags of potato chips and a bottle of Coke.

Somewhere beyond Newburg I dozed off, and when I woke up the train was standing in the station at Springfield. The conductor announced that the Springfield stop would be for thirty minutes, but this time I stayed on the train and looked out the window. While we were at the depot, two other trains, one from Kansas City and one from Memphis, pulled in. For a few minutes the platform was crowded with people collecting their luggage and greeting friends and family who had come to meet them. Some, who were making connections in Springfield, boarded our train.

Later, as we neared Afton, I started to worry. In my hurry to get packed up to go, I hadn't really stopped to think about what things were going to be like in Fairweather. Now I was having serious concerns. Grandmother and Granddad were sure to have questions that I might not be able to answer. What if they somehow blamed Mom and me for what happened to Dad? What was I going to do down here? And then I started thinking about other stuff, like what was Wendy going to think about how I never called her back? Maybe I could call her from Fairweather. I thought I could offer to pay Grandmother for the cost of the long-distance call.

And then I thought about my father, and I realized that more than anything, I was angry with him. I knew it was selfish, but I couldn't help thinking that all of this was his fault. I remembered Mom said the accident might have been the result of the medicine he was taking and not that he had been drinking, but I also knew that if he had cared more about Mom and me and less about himself, maybe none of this would have happened.

If he died, I thought, *this would all be over, and I could just go home.*

The train rounded a curve, and a moment later the conductor came into the car and called "Afton, next. Afton, Oklahoma, will be the next stop."

When I felt the train slowing down, I got up

from my seat and pulled my suitcase from the
overhead rack. A minute later the train squealed to
a stop. The conductor opened the door and I stepped
down onto the platform. Up ahead I could see the
rest of my luggage being handed down from the
baggage car to the depot agent, who piled it on a
cart along with some other suitcases and several
Railway Express packages. A minute or so went by,
a few more people boarded and then the train began
to move. As the last car passed me by, I looked up
and down the platform expecting to see
Grandmother and Granddad, but instead I saw that I
was being met by absolutely no one.

CHAPTER SIX:

Getting Reacquainted

I collected my suitcases and golf clubs and took a seat on the bench outside the waiting room. A few other people had gotten off along with me, and they either walked to their cars in the parking lot or else met friends or relatives who had showed up to greet them. Within ten minutes I was by myself.

A short time later the station agent came out to where I was sitting.

"Excuse me, but are you figuring on somebody coming to pick you up?"

"My grandparents," I said. "They're driving up from Fairweather."

"Reason I ask," he said, "is, the *Meteor* ain't due in either direction until after midnight, so I generally lock up and go home 'til around ten-thirty. You think you'll be okay here by yourself?"

The *Meteor* was the Frisco's night train between St. Louis and Oklahoma City. "I'll be fine. I guess maybe they just lost track of time. They should be along in a few minutes."

"Okay, then. There's a phone booth around on the other side of the depot, in case you need to make a call," he said, and hiked off in the direction of town.

I sat there for another hour, during which time a freight train went past in either direction. Then an old Buick that I recognized as my grandmother's car pulled into the parking lot and my Uncle Bob got out.

Uncle Bob looked about the same as I remembered him from the last time our family had visited. He was skinny, not tall, with dark hair and a thin face, like Dad looked in pictures taken when he was a kid. He wore tight blue jeans and a plaid short-sleeved shirt, white socks and black shoes. His hair was on the long side and slicked back with hair tonic, and he had a pair of Ray-Ban sunglasses propped up on top of his head. As he walked up, he stuck out his hand for me to shake.

"Sorry I'm late. I had something I been needing to do, and today was the day."

"That's okay," I said, taking his hand. "How've you been?"

"Not too bad, I guess." He picked up my golf clubs and one of the suitcases. "How's your dad?"

"Not too good, or I wouldn't be here."

"I guess not," he said. "What happened, anyway?"

I shrugged. "He got drunk. He crashed into a phone pole. He got hurt. That's what drunks do."

"Can he talk?"

"He can't do anything. When you're with him, it's like neither one of you is even in the room."

"I can imagine." Bob flicked his hand at a bug buzzing around in front of his face. "I heard his doctor is a nigger."

His words surprised me. I'd heard the term before, of course, and, I am not proud to admit, even used it myself when I was hanging around with my friends. But neither Mom nor Dad had ever said it when I was in earshot. I wondered, since Bob had obviously gotten his information from Grandmother, why Mom had thought to mention it when she called to arrange my coming down.

"One of his doctors is colored, yes. He's supposed to be very good."

"It seems like to me they could have found somebody else if they wanted to."

Bob helped me load my stuff into the trunk of the Buick. When we were back on the highway headed toward Fairweather he said, "If your grandmother asks, the train was late, okay?"

"Bob," I said, "that train takes nine hours to go three hundred and forty miles. The only way it could be late is if it fell off the tracks."

"Just the same," he told me. He took a pack of cigarettes out of his shirt pocket and shook it in my direction. "Want a smoke?"

"No thanks," I told him. He stuck one in his mouth and lit it.

"You don't smoke? What are you, still in diapers?"

"No. I tried it once, and I didn't like it. Anyway, I'm going out for the golf team at school this fall, and you have to sign a pledge that you won't smoke if you're on a team."

"I thought golf was a game for old farts. Do you figure the coach is going to know what you were doing while you were in Oklahoma?"

So far I didn't seem to be getting any right answers. "I figure I'll know, Bob."

"Uh-huh. Did your mama give you any indication how much time you might be spending down here?"

"I don't think she knows. Until Dad gets better, I guess."

"Well," Bob said, "let's hope for both of us that ain't too long."

Grandmother's car was the same one I remembered she had when we had visited two years earlier: a four-door 1949 Buick, called a Roadmaster, painted a shade of green that looked like pea soup. It had wide whitewall tires and bumpers big enough to turn on their sides and use as canoes. For being as old as it was, though, it was in perfect shape. The paint gleamed, and the seat covers and floor mats were spotless. I remembered that although Granddad didn't drive, it was his special pleasure to go out on Saturday mornings to wash and wax the car.

The Buick didn't start like any other car I'd ever seen. You had to turn the key in the ignition then push the gas pedal all the way to the floor. That engaged the starter, which fired up a big eight-cylinder engine. It had an automatic transmission called a Hydra-matic, which let the car accelerate smoothly, but very gradually, like starting a train. The Buick was big, heavy and quiet, and looked as if it had been designed for people who weren't in any hurry to get where they were going. It was definitely not a young man's car.

On the drive back to Fairweather Bob asked a few more questions about Dad and I told him what I knew. Once or twice he looked over at me and stared real hard, like he was trying to make out some resemblance to Dad in my face.

After a while Bob ran out of questions, so he turned on the radio and more or less ignored me the rest of the way back to Fairweather. I decided that was fine with me. I was tired of the whole conversation. I rolled the window down and watched the green fields glide by. The air smelled rich, with a mixture of moist earth and young plants seemingly sprouting and blossoming everywhere. Even though it was past six-thirty, the sun was still high in the sky and the combination of the late afternoon light reflecting off the Buick's hood and the soft hum of the tires on the pavement caused me to close my eyes and drift into a deep sleep.

*   *   *   *

My grandparents lived in an old one-story house in a part of town called Royal Heights. The name was misleading, as no one living there was apt to have come from royalty. At one time my grandparents had owned close to fifty acres and used it to maintain a family farm. During the Depression, and later, during World War II when many food items were rationed, they grew vegetables, which Grandmother cooked and put up for the winter. They also had a couple of cows and a chicken coop, so there was always fresh milk and eggs. Grandmother said that the extra food came in handy, especially since she and Granddad were raising four boys on Granddad's salary as a Railway Express agent. But after my father and my uncles were grown and had moved away from home, they began selling off the land so that by the time Bob, who came along much later and was a surprise to everyone, was growing up they were down to just a few acres. All that was left of the farm was a big vegetable patch and the chicken coop, which still furnished eggs and an occasional fryer for Sunday supper.

The land that Grandmother and Granddad sold off had been taken over by developers who put in gravel streets and small, cheaply constructed houses. As far as I knew, my grandparents didn't socialize with any of their neighbors, and on more than a few occasions I heard my Grandmother refer to them as "white trash." She always said that if she had known the kind of people who were going to wind up being her neighbors, she never would have agreed to sell.

Bob and I got back to Fairweather a little after seven. Instead of opening the gate and pulling into the side yard, Bob left the Buick parked on the street in front of the house. I took that to mean he would be going out later. Grandmother's eyesight was not the best, and she hardly ever drove her car after dark.

Grandmother and Granddad were sitting on the glider swing on their big front porch waiting for us. As Bob and I unloaded my luggage from the trunk they came down the walk to meet us. Grandmother was leading the way.

"Bob, you're late," she said. "I expected you back here near to an hour ago."

Bob looked at me, and I knew that was my cue. "The train was late, Grandmother," I said. "We got held for a freight train in Monett for almost an hour."

"No, you didn't," she said, looking straight at Bob. "I called down to the depot at Vinita before I put supper on the stove, so it would be ready when you two got here. Agent there said it was on time." She turned her gaze to me. "And there ain't any call for you to be telling tales for this scamp, leastways not before you get your suitcase unpacked."

She turned back to Bob, poking him in the chest with her finger. "Look here, until you get that scrap heap of yours running, if you want to use my car for whatever foolishness you got going on, you do it when you ain't out running errands for me. Now take the boy's things inside and wash up for supper."

"Aw, Ma, I was planning to go see Bonnie."

"You'll have a proper supper before you go anyplace, and that's all there is to it."

Bob looked like he wanted to argue with her, but I knew as well as he did there was no such thing as winning an argument with Grandmother. He managed to gather my two suitcases in one hand and my duffel bag and golf clubs in the other and stagger up the front steps into the house.

Grandmother turned her attention back to me. She hugged me once up against her big body, then put her hands on my shoulders and held me at arm's length.

"Well let's have a look at you, boy. What's it been, two, three years?"

"I guess so, Grandmother. I missed you and Granddad."

She nodded once. "You look good. Now come on inside and get washed up for supper and then we can sit and talk for a spell. Granddad and I have a lot of questions, but then I expect you already figured that."

"Yes, ma'am," I said.

Granddad, who up to that point hadn't said anything, finally took his pipe out of his mouth and smiled. "It's good to see you, Gary. We're just as sorry as can be it had to be this way."

Bob put my stuff in the middle of the three bedrooms that ran along one side of the house. The room was nothing fancy. There were two single beds, one up against each wall, and a chest of drawers next to the door. I knew from my earlier visits that this was the room my father had shared with my Uncle Ronald when they were growing up three decades earlier. I also knew that Uncle Ronald, being older than Dad, had laid claim to the bed nearest the window because in the hot Oklahoma summer, being close to the window made for better sleeping. However, except for a photo of each of them that had been taken during their senior years in high school, there wasn't anything in the room that indicated either of them had ever slept there.

I chose Uncle Ronald's bed to sleep in and laid out my suitcases and my duffel bag on the other bed. I stowed my golf clubs in the back of the closet. Then, having nothing else to do, I sat down on the bed to wait until it was time for supper.

CHAPTER SEVEN:
Bob's Big News

Grandmother had prepared a delicious supper, as she always did when family came to visit. Tonight, it was pork chops, mashed potatoes and green beans, and if the meal had somehow suffered from having to wait in the oven for an extra hour, I didn't notice. As I remembered was her habit when she was feeding family rather than guests, we ate around the kitchen table rather than the big walnut table in her dining room.

Bob might have been in a hurry to get going, but he ate everything on his plate. I knew he had someplace he wanted to go, but he had the good sense not to rush through his meal. Grandmother did not take kindly to bad manners at her supper table.

After the dishes were cleared, she served each of us a slice of cherry pie.

"I know this is your favorite," she said to me, "so I made it special. Now don't go figurin' on this every night, because I ain't in the habit, but since this is your first night, I'm glad to do it."

Over dessert Grandmother and Granddad peppered me with questions about Dad, and I tried my best to fill them in on his condition. It was hard for me to keep answering because I could give them almost no positive news apart from the fact that he was in good hands in a good hospital. When I told them how he looked, I saw my grandmother wipe a tear from the corner of her eye. Granddad didn't say too much; he just kept turning his coffee cup around and around, as if he was trying to screw it into the top of the table. Bob sat quietly through the entire conversation. I knew that had to be hard since he was in a hurry to get going and I had already told him what I knew during the ride back from Afton.

At last, when it seemed as if they had run

out of questions, Granddad said, "I hate to ask you this, Gary, but has your dad started drinking again?"

Maybe it was the tone of Granddad's voice, or maybe it was the look on my grandmother's face, but there was only one way I was going to answer that question.

"No, Granddad," I lied. "He stopped a long time ago."

After supper, while Bob helped with the dishes, I went into the guest bedroom and began unpacking my suitcases. Over the sound of water running from the kitchen faucet I could hear Grandmother and Bob talking. I didn't get all of it, but the conversation seemed to have something to do with Bob's plans for the night. At one point I heard Bob say, "Aw, Ma," and then my grandmother said "Well, that's how it is. If that don't suit you, then you can just walk."

A minute or so later, as I was hanging up the last of my clothes in the closet, Bob appeared in the doorway.

"Come on," he said, "get cleaned up if you

need to and let's get to going."

Five minutes later, after I had washed my face and combed my hair we were back in the Buick. "Where are we going?" I asked. "And what's the hurry?"

"We're going into town to meet up with some friends."

I said, "By 'friends,' are we talking somebody named Bonnie?'"

"There'll be others, but that's right," Bob said.

"And then what?"

"And then hang out for a while. See what's going on."

"What's that got to do with me?" I asked. "Why do I need to go along?"

"You don't," he said. "And that's what I told your grandmother. But she said either I was to take you with me or else I couldn't use the car. 'Course that won't be a problem once I get that Chevy in the side yard running."

I had noticed an old Chevrolet sedan parked next to my grandparents' house when Bob and I arrived from the train station. It was painted in gray primer, and the hood was up. From the weeds that were growing up through the engine compartment, it was obvious that, whatever the Chevy had going for it, one of those things was most definitely not an engine.

"It's a '51, in case you don't recognize it," Bob said. "Tomorrow I'm heading up to Kansas City to pick up a 409 engine your Uncle Warren found for me. But for the minute," he looked at me like I was chewing gum on the bottom of his shoe, "I've got no car of my own, so I guess I'm stuck with you."

That did it. I said, "Stop the car."

"What?"

"Stop the damn car. Do it now!"

Bob pulled the Buick over to the curb. "What's the matter now? Are you sick?"

"Yeah, I'm sick," I said. "I'm sick of you, already." I looked at him. "Ever since I got off the train you've made it clear that me being here is a huge problem for you. Well let me tell you, I didn't ask to come down here and I didn't ask to come along with you tonight."

"Now wait just a dang minute," he began.

"No, you wait," I said, getting angrier as I went along. "I should be home right now with my mom and dad and my friends, but I can't, and there's nothing I can do about it. You might be stuck with me, but I'm stuck with you, too, and if you think my idea of a good time is hanging around some hamburger stand with you and a bunch of your redneck friends, well, think again. So you can just drop me off someplace where there's a phone and I'll call a cab and go on back to the house. Tomorrow you can run me back to Afton and I'll figure out what to tell Mom when I get home, because I am not going to listen to you complaining every minute we're together."

Bob gave a loud sigh. He leaned forward and hung his arms over the steering wheel. "Look, Gary, I'm sorry about what I said. 'Course I'm glad to see you and I'm happy you're here. My being cranky ain't got anything to do with you, but I've had a hell of a day. So, if you can just back off a little, I promise tomorrow will be better, okay?"

I thought about what Mom would say if I unexpectedly turned up back home on tomorrow's train, and I knew that she would not be happy. Like it or not, I was going to be in Fairweather for a while, so there was nothing to do except make the best of it. Not that Bob needed to know that, although I suspected he knew I was running a bluff.

"Okay," I said, "I've had a hell of a last few days myself, so I apologize for the outburst. You already know about what's going on with me, so tell me about your day and then we'll be even."

Bob shook a cigarette out of his pack, lit it and inhaled deeply, "You got to swear on your life that what I'm about to tell you will stay right here in this car."

I figured he was going to tell me something stupid, like he got a speeding ticket on the way to

Afton, although driving the Buick I couldn't
imagine how.

"Not a word," I said. "I promise."

"Well, the reason I was late picking you up
at the train station is that I went down today and
joined the Marines."

I nearly jumped out of my seat. "You did
what?"

"That's right. It'll be official soon as I turn
eighteen, which will be seventy-seven days from
right now."

"But you're not finished with high school,
are you? Don't you have another year to go?"

"Yeah, but I'm just wastin' time, Gary,"
Bob said. "I sit in them classes every day listening
to them teachers and not understanding anything
they're talkin' about. School ain't the place for me.
Besides, the sergeant down at the recruiting station
said the Marine Corps would give me training in
whatever field I wanted. I told them I wanted to be
an aircraft mechanic, and they said that was great

because they can use all the mechanics they could get."

"I'm sure they can," I said, "in Vietnam. Why do you think they were in such a hurry to get you signed up?"

"Makes no difference," Bob said. "Being smart and from the city you wouldn't know this, but for somebody like me who ain't got enough upstairs to go to college there aren't but two ways out of this town. One is to go to prison, which I certainly am not going to do. The other is to join the service, which is what I did. And if you're a man of your word like I hope you are, you won't say anything about this to your Grandmother."

"She'll never hear it from me," I said. "Is there anything else?"

"Well, yeah, there's Bonnie," Bob took a last drag on his cigarette and threw the butt out the window. "When I see her tonight, I'm going to ask her to marry me."

CHAPTER EIGHT:

Gideon

In Fairweather, Oklahoma, "going into town" mostly consisted of driving back and forth between Skelley's Drive-In on the north end of Kansas Avenue and the A&W Root Beer stand on the south end. The primary activities seemed to be hanging around with other kids, eating "wets," which were French fries with gravy poured over them, drinking cherry cokes and chocolate phosphates, and sometimes heading out to the River Road to watch drag races that had been set up earlier in the evening.

"So how come we didn't pick up Bonnie on the way into town?" I asked Bob as we pulled into the A&W lot. "I mean, if you're going to ask her to get married, shouldn't you at least give her a ride to the engagement party?"

"I can't exactly do that. Her daddy and me, we don't see eye to eye on a number of things," Bob answered.

"Like first and foremost, you dating his daughter?"

"That would be top of the list," Bob agreed.

We pulled into the A&W lot and found a parking spot for the Buick. Bob introduced me to some of his friends, including Lee Lathrop and Rabbit Miles, his best friends from high school. Lee was a muscular-looking kid who had football player written all over him. He was built low to the ground with wide shoulders and thick, powerful-looking arms. His hair was cut short and he had the beginnings of a beard growing on his chin. On the other hand, Rabbit was small and skinny and looked more like a sixth grader than a high school junior. He had stringy blond hair and blue eyes that darted from side to side as he talked. Both Lee and Rabbit lived right down the road from my grandparents, so the three of them had more or less grown up together.

"There's gonna be a race later on," Lee told Bob and me excitedly. "Jack Swimmer put an 850 double-pumper on his Corvette and he's taking on Dave Bethune in his Max-Wedge Plymouth. We're all heading out about ten-thirty. Word is they've got fifty dollars on it."

Now *that* sounded interesting. There was a Beach Boys song called "Shut Down" about two guys racing, one in a Corvette, and the other in a Dodge, which is just like a Plymouth. In the song the Corvette wins, but I had my doubts about how a race like that might actually turn out. Either way, I was definitely up for being there.

Bob introduced me to a few more people, including a pretty girl named Rhonda, who I later found out had just about the richest parents in northeast Oklahoma. But even without knowing that, I could tell right away she was somebody special from the number of other kids who were hanging around her. Rhonda's girlfriend was named

Paulette. Like Rhonda, Paulette appeared to be very much a member of Fairweather's in-crowd. However, unlike Rhonda, who didn't seem to be attached to anybody in particular, Paulette was glued to the right arm of a guy named Albert.

Albert was about the size of a Coca-Cola machine, built like Lee but much taller. He let go of Paulette long enough to shake my hand, then wrapped his arm back around her shoulder. The move reminded me of a film I saw once in our biology class that showed how animals mark their territory by putting their scent all over it.

While I stood wondering what to do next, Bob moved off to talk to Rhonda. A minute later he came back and asked if I would be all right by myself for a few minutes while he drove over to Skelley's to pick up Bonnie. Apparently, they had gotten their wires crossed earlier in the day and she and Bob had wound up at different ends of the strip. Lee said I could ride with him and Rabbit out to the race later, so I told Bob to go ahead and do whatever he had to do.

It had been a long day, and I was beginning to feel the weight of it, so rather than stand around trying to make conversation with a lot of people I had only just met, I walked over to a cluster of picnic tables at one end of the parking lot and sat down. As my mind drifted back over the events of the last couple of days, I noticed a boy staring at me from across the parking lot. Not sure whether I had met him earlier, I waved and smiled in his direction. He waved back and walked over to where I was sitting.

"You're Gary, right?" he asked.

"I'm sorry," I said. "Did I meet you earlier?"

"No. I heard some of the other kids talking and I thought I'd come over and say hello. My name is Gideon."

He was about the same age as Bob's other friends, sixteen or seventeen, but he was dressed a little differently. Instead of blue jeans or white Levis, he wore navy blue dress slacks, and instead of sneakers, polished leather shoes. And although it was a very warm evening, he wore a sweater over a white dress shirt. I guessed he must have just gotten off work someplace where the air conditioning was turned on high.

"I hear you're going to be spending the summer here in Fairweather," he said.

"I don't know about the whole summer," I said. "My dad is sick, and my mom wanted me out of the way until things settle down at home."

"Yes, that's what I heard some of the others saying."

That surprised me. "People are talking about me?"

"It's a small town. Word gets around. For now, you're the news." He spoke in a quiet voice that made him sound a lot more grown up than he looked.

"Are you one of Bob's friends?" I asked.

"I know Bob. I wouldn't say we're friends. But I was thinking maybe you and I could be friends, at least for the time you're here visiting."

Well, why not, I thought. This guy seemed a little odd, and the way he was asking me to be friends sounded like the way a guy asks a girl to go on a date, but having at least one person to talk to was probably better than hanging around a drive-in restaurant with a bunch of strangers every night.

"Sure," I said, "let's be friends. Do you play golf by any chance?"

He smiled. "Sorry, no. But there might be other things we can do."

"Okay," I said, trying to imagine what those might be. Maybe we could go door to door handing out religious pamphlets or collecting old clothes for a charity drive. My first impression was that Gideon was not the type to go in for anything much more exciting than that.

Just then I heard a car horn. I looked in the direction of the sound and saw Lee waving at me. All over the A&W parking lot kids were getting into their cars and heading out. It was time to go racing. I started to tell Gideon maybe I'd see him later, but he was gone. I didn't know how he could have disappeared so quickly, but I had looked away when Lee honked and supposed Gideon had just melted into the crowd of kids and cars.

Lee was already in his car revving the engine when I walked back across the parking lot. Rabbit was in the back seat, looking none too happy about it.

"You ready to go?" Lee asked. "Rabbit usually rides shotgun, but I told him you could sit up front this trip. Now that you been in that Buick your Grandmother's got, I'll show you what a real ride is like."

Lee's car was a '58 Ford painted red with black wheels and no hubcaps. The chrome trim had all been removed and the car had been lowered a couple of inches on its suspension, giving it the appearance of a race car. I couldn't tell what kind of an engine he had, but whatever was under the hood rumbled dangerously out of a pair of three-inch exhaust pipes that exited just behind the rear wheels.

Lee guessed what I was thinking. "It's a 430 cubic inch Interceptor V8 out of a 1960

Thunderbird. I bought it at a junkyard in Tulsa for two hundred dollars. Soon as I can save up another hundred, I'm getting a four-speed transmission to go along with it. Even with a three-speed, though, this baby runs like a scalded ape." He grinned and gunned the engine to make sure I hadn't missed the point.

"Fasten your seatbelts, boys. We are going to the races."

Kansas Avenue, the main street through Fairweather, is U.S. Highway 69, which becomes a divided four-lane just south of town. About five miles past the city limits the highway starts to run parallel to the Neosho River. At that point the four-lane diverges from what I learned was the original highway, now called River Road. The highway department built the new alignment after the Neosho flooded three times in four years, each time washing out parts of the pavement. The new highway was built on higher ground, while the old road was patched up with blacktop. Now the only people who used it were the few people who lived along the river and fishermen who used the boat ramp at the far end of it. Because there was a stretch of the River Road that ran straight for about half a mile, it also made a perfect drag strip.

On the way out of town, I turned in my seat to face Rabbit. "I've been wanting to ask you. Did your mom and dad really name you Rabbit?"

Lee answered with a laugh. "Naw, his real name is Woodrow. We call him Rabbit, because, well, me and your uncle and Woodrow, we were shopping for watermelons in a farmer's field a few years back, and the farmer's dog heard what we were up to and took out running after us. Woodrow, he ran so fast even the dog couldn't catch him. After that the name just seemed to fit."

"Got it," I said.

By the time we got to the River Road drag strip most of the kids from Skelley's and the A&W had already arrived and were parked along the side of the road across from the river. Along the side nearest the river there was only a narrow shoulder and a wooden guard rail that didn't look sturdy enough to keep a car from crashing through into the river if the road were icy or if a driver lost control.

A few cars ahead of where Lee had parked his Ford I saw Bob holding hands with a pretty girl. I guessed that must be Bonnie. I couldn't see either of their faces well enough to make a guess as to whether Bob had made his proposal yet, or if he had what her answer had been. I decided now was as good a time as any to meet the girl who might end up being my future aunt, so I walked over to where they were standing. Even in flat shoes, Bonnie was nearly as tall as Bob. She wore a sleeveless summer dress and her hair hung down past her shoulders.

Bob tried to ignore me at first, but when it became obvious I wasn't going to go away, he said, "Bonnie, this here is my nephew Gary. He's going to be staying with us for a while until his daddy gets out of the hospital."

"Hello, Gary," Bonnie said, and she gave me a smile that made me instantly like her. "Bob said his nephew was coming, but I got the impression he was talking about somebody a lot younger. I had no idea you were so grown up."

"Actually, Bob and I are about three years apart," I said.

"Well, that's not so much. Bob and I are only a year apart ourselves, which makes you pretty close to the same age as some of my friends." She turned to Bob. "We'll have to introduce Gary to some of my girlfriends while he's here." She turned back to me. "You wouldn't mind meeting some girls while you're here, would you?"

"I guess not. Sure, why not?" I said. I stood there for a minute not knowing what else to say. Bob caught my eye and started making small but insistent movements with his head. I got the message.

"Well, I'd better get back to Lee and Rabbit. They're my ride tonight. It was nice meeting you, Bonnie."

"Nice meeting you, Gary. See you again soon."

So now I had met Bonnie, and I still had no idea whether she was in line to be part of the family, or if Bob had even asked her yet if she wanted to be. I wondered what it would be like to have an aunt who was almost close enough to my own age to ask to a high school dance as my date.

I drifted back over to where a group of guys were standing around arguing about which car was likely to be faster. Rabbit saw me staring at a white stripe somebody had painted across both lanes of the road.

"That there is the starting line. A quarter mile down is the finish. A couple of the guys came out here one day and measured it off exactly. This is as good a drag strip as you'll find anyplace in the county."

"Unless somebody goes into the river," I said.

"I guess that's so," Rabbit agreed. "They'll be doing better than a hundred and twenty by the time they get to the finish."

"No way," Lee said, and I knew he was right. At home I read lots of car magazines and I knew that neither the Plymouth nor the Corvette would be able to get much over a hundred by the end of a quarter mile unless they had been completely rebuilt as race cars. And if they had been they would be almost impossible to drive on the street, and probably illegal as well.

"You got your own car yet, Gary?" Rabbit asked.

"I'm fifteen, Rabbit," I said, adding a couple of months to my real age. "I don't even have a learner's permit yet."

"So then you don't even know how to drive. Have you ever been in a car that went more than a hundred?"

Actually, the answer to that was yes, I did, and yes, I had.

*   *   *   *

It was last year in September. Dad had just gotten a promotion at the railroad. He decided to celebrate by buying himself a new car. It was a yellow Mustang convertible, which he had been talking about getting ever since they had come on the market at the beginning of the year. He was very proud of it and had started teaching me to drive on Sunday afternoons when we could find an empty parking lot for me to use as a practice course.

One night about three months after he bought the car we got into a discussion that turned into an argument and I told him I thought the Mustang sucked because he had ordered it with a six-cylinder engine instead of a more powerful V8. I don't know why I said it except that he had been drinking that night after he promised he was going to quit. That made me mad, so I tried to get back at him the only way I could, with words that I knew would hurt him.

He said let's see if this car has a big enough engine, and he tossed me the keys and said we're going for a ride, with me driving. He told me to head out to the Interstate and then to go ahead and floor it and we'll see what quits first, the car or me. He was drunk, and I knew I should have just refused to go with him. But then I thought, okay, I'll show you, and I stood on the gas until we were going about a hundred and ten. At that speed, the car felt like an airplane trying to lift off the runway, but I finally wrung every bit of speed out of it.

When we got to the next exit ramp, I peeled off the Interstate and turned the car around. Then I drove us home, keeping ten miles under the speed limit the entire way. When we got back to the house I pulled the car into the driveway and turned off the engine. I handed him back the keys and said, "I had it backwards. There's nothing wrong with this car. There's something wrong with you." Not until I got back into the house did I realize that I was crying uncontrollably.

Neither of us ever said another word about that night.

*   *   *   *

We stood around for about twenty minutes waiting for the two guys who were going to race to get their cars ready. I decided I'd rather see the finish and walked the quarter mile down the road to the other end of the course. There was another white stripe painted on the pavement and another group of kids waiting for the race to start. Finally, we heard engines revving, followed by the sound of tires squealing and then two pairs of headlights quickly approaching in the distance.

As I had expected, the Corvette was light in the back end. The big new carburetor was letting the engine deliver more horsepower than the rear wheels could keep on the ground. As a result, the 'Vette couldn't get traction and the Plymouth won going away.

After the big race a few other cars squared off against one another, and before the evening was over I had watched maybe a dozen races, including Lee, who outran somebody in a Pontiac. By the end of the night Bob and Bonnie were nowhere to be found, and so Lee offered to drive me back to the A&W or to my Grandmother's house if that was what I wanted. I looked at my watch and saw it was nearly one-thirty. I told Lee I'd had enough for one day and asked him to take me home.

CHAPTER NINE:
Lewis Tate

The next day was Saturday. Bob had to be up early because he and Lee were driving to Kansas City to pick up a Chevrolet 409 engine that he planned to install in the car he had been building in the side yard.

"I'd take you along, but we're going in Lee's daddy's pickup, and it'd be a bit crowded with three of us in the cab. Besides, we're gonna do an all-nighter so we can be back by late tomorrow morning. Think you can get along for one day without me lookin' over your shoulder?"

"I can manage," I told him.

As it ended up, it was another long day. Bob

and Lee left about the time the sun was coming up
and the noise Bob made getting out of the house
woke me up, so after Bob and Lee took off, I was
stuck with nothing to do and a whole day in which
to do it.

After breakfast, Granddad put me to work
mowing the lawn. That wasn't too bad, because he
had a garden tractor which at least meant I didn't
have to spend the day walking around behind a
power mower getting pounded by the blistering
Oklahoma sun.

That evening, Uncle Ronald and Aunt
Virginia took me out to dinner. Uncle Ronald was a
couple of years older than Dad, and he and Aunt
Virginia had a lot of questions about how Dad was
doing and what did I think were his chances for
recovery. I wished I could have told tell them
something good, and I could see the worry in Uncle
Ronald's face as I went back over all that had
happened. After dinner we all went to a movie
called *Girl Happy*. It was an Elvis Presley picture
set in Hawaii, and I guess they thought since I was a

kid I must be an Elvis fan. On the way home, Aunt Virginia asked me whether I enjoyed the movie and I said it was really great, but the truth was, it sucked. Even the songs were bad.

The next morning Grandmother and Granddad took me to church. I hadn't really thought about the possibility of that when I was packing, but I did have a pair of dark slacks and a white shirt. Granddad loaned me a tie and we found one of Bob's sport coats that more or less fit and away we went. I sat in the front with Grandmother; Granddad sat in the back.

In the car I asked Grandmother what the name of her parish was, and I was surprised when she said the church was called Our Savior, and that it was a Lutheran church.

I said, "Grandmother, I don't think I should go with you today."

"Well, for heaven's sake, why not?"

I hesitated, not sure how to answer without upsetting her. "It's like this. At our religious instruction, Sister told us that there are two kinds of people in the world. There are Catholics and there are pagans. They said that if a Catholic goes to a pagan Sunday service it doesn't count the same as going to mass, and missing mass is a mortal sin. That means if a Catholic skips mass and then dies before he can go to Confession and get absolution, he'll wind up in hell for all eternity."

"So, your idea is that Granddad and I are pagans?" With that question, I knew I was treading on dangerous ground. "Is that what you believe about your Granddad and me? We're going to spend eternity in the fiery pit of hell?"

"I don't think that, Grandmother. Sister Mary Agnes does."

"I never heard of such a foolish thing," Grandmother said. "There are millions of people all over the world who don't go to Catholic churches. If what you're saying is right, there ain't a hell big enough to hold all of us."

"Tell that to Sister," I said, but it was Granddad who came to the rescue.

"Tell you what we'll do. Let's go ahead and go on to services. We might just as well since we're already here. Then next week, if you still don't feel right about things, we'll go to the Catholic service. We can call it an even trade. You go to our church today and we'll go to yours next time. Will that be okay?"

Of course, that was perfectly okay with me. The fact was, at home we hardly ever went to church on Sunday, although Mom did make sure I attended religious instruction on Monday nights during the school year. And although I didn't really believe that I would go to hell for walking into a Lutheran church, I did have it in the back of my head that God might take it out on Dad because I hadn't obeyed the nuns. It was stupid, I know, but taking chances with God was something I wasn't sure I wanted to do just then. But then again, Granddad was right. I really didn't have a choice.

I have to say this much: My grandparents' church certainly did not look like the doorway to hell. The building itself was huge, and it reminded me of pictures I had seen in my history books of cathedrals in Europe. It was built of gray limestone and sat on a corner just off Kansas Avenue. Wide granite steps led up to a set of heavy, carved wooden doors, and there were stained glass windows twice as tall as a man on every side. For some reason, when Grandmother had told me earlier that we were going to church, I imagined a small building out in the country, but this church was as big as the main cathedral in St. Louis.

I got another surprise when we went inside. A lot of people came over and greeted Grandmother and Granddad, and Grandmother introduced me to each of them. After I shook hands with what seemed like half the population of Fairweather, it became very clear that my grandparents were both well-known and highly respected in town. The biggest surprise, though, was that when we were ushered to our seats we were in a pew that had a shiny brass nameplate on the end of it. The nameplate read "Donated by Edward and Sophia Seiler."

But how could that be? My grandparents had a car that was older than me, a house on a street that wasn't even paved and yet they had a pew with their names on it in what had to be the biggest church for a hundred miles around.

The service ran longer than a Catholic mass, and it was different in many ways from what I was used to. For one thing, there was no kneeling. People stood up, people sat down, but nobody ever knelt down. In fact, they couldn't if they wanted to as there were no kneelers attached to the pews. For another, there was a lot more singing, and everything was in English instead of some parts being in Latin. Finally, the communion ceremony was not at all like at home. In a Catholic church, you kneel at the altar and receive communion from the priest, who places the communion wafer on your tongue. In this church, baskets containing small pieces of bread were passed down the row from one person to another. Right behind came a small tray that held tiny cups of wine. Of course, I didn't dare take any of either. For one thing I wasn't a member of this church and didn't think I was entitled to do so. For another, there was still Sister Mary Agnes.

The theme of the pastor's sermon was forgiveness. His point seemed to be that the path to spiritual peace was directly connected to the ability to move beyond whatever wrongs might have been done to us in the past. There were moments, as he spoke, that I got the feeling he was talking about Dad and me.

After the service was over, Grandmother and Granddad took me to breakfast at a downtown restaurant. While we were waiting for a table I got to meet a lot more people, and again to my surprise, most of the people were approaching my grandparents and not the other way around. I made up my mind to find out what that was all about the first chance I got.

When we returned home from lunch (my grandparents called it "dinner"), Bob and Lee were back from Kansas City. Lee had pulled his pickup close to the garage and he and Bob were unloading the new engine. They had rigged up the frame from a metal swing set with a chain hoist and were slowly lifting the big engine clear of the bed of the truck. As I watched, they lowered it onto a homemade engine stand built from two-by-four and four-by-four lumber. The stand had wheels attached to the bottom, so that the engine could be rolled into the garage once it was set squarely down. Grandmother finished parking the car and went into the house. Granddad and I walked back to check out the operation.

"It's out of a '61 Impala Super Sport," Bob announced proudly. "It's only got about twenty thousand miles on it. The guy that had it before put the car into the side of a highway overpass. Killed himself instantly is what the junkyard man said."

Granddad looked the operation over skeptically. "See to it you don't do the same," he said, and then he went into the house. I followed him in to change out of my church clothes.

When I came back out, Bob and Lee were already in the garage and had started taking the engine apart. They had pulled off the rocker arm covers and dropped the oil pan, allowing what oil was left in the crankcase to drip out onto the bare ground in front of the garage. There wasn't any way to actually start it, since there was no battery, no radiator and, since it wasn't fastened down yet, no way to keep it from flying right off the wooden engine stand if they did get it going. But Lee said he could tell by looking inside the engine whether it was going to need any work before it went into the car, or if it was okay the way it was.

Lee was down in the dirt, lying on his back, peering up into the engine. He had a flashlight in one hand and a tool that looked something like a small pocket knife with about twenty blades in the other.

"You know what he's doing?" Bob asked me.

"Checking the crankshaft end-play," I said.

Lee whistled. "The kid knows something about engines. I'm impressed."

"I read a lot of car magazines," I said. I was trying to sound cool, but it actually felt pretty good to get Lee's approval. "Plus, my dad and I took apart our lawn mower engine last summer, so I got a look at what was in there. All engines work basically the same."

"Oh, yeah, your dad," said Lee. "Any word on how he's doing?"

"About like he was, I guess. I haven't heard anything from my mom since I got here, and I'm pretty sure she would have called if there was anything good to tell me."

"Probably," Lee said. "Too bad about his doctor, though. Bob told me the guy was a, well, he ain't a regular doctor. You'd think in a big city like St. Louis, they could have found somebody better."

"What are we talking about here," I asked, "whether he's any good as a doctor or the fact that he's colored?"

Lee went back to fiddling inside the engine. "Well, ain't it all pretty much the same thing?"

I thought back to the feeling I had when I met Dr. Oswald at the hospital. I had to ask myself whether my own ideas were really all that much different from Lee's.

"It might have been, once, but times are changing," I said. "Look at what happened when all those people demonstrated in Washington a couple of years ago, and what Martin Luther King is doing now. Dad says there's going to be another civil rights law passed this year. We've got a few colored kids in our school, and from what I hear, there are a bunch more at the high school I'll be going to next year."

Lee and Bob stared at me like I was talking in some foreign language.

I said, "Are you telling me you don't have any colored kids at your school?"

"Don't know of any," Lee said. "Of course, that ain't because the school is segregated. It's just that we've got two high schools here in Fairweather, and, well, whites and coloreds pretty much have always each had their own schools. It's just how the district boundaries are set up."

"And does that seem okay to you?" I asked.

"I don't know why not." Lee dropped his wrench on the ground and sat up. "Understand, I ain't saying there's anything wrong with colored people exactly, it's just that things are a little different down here. Up north, you've got big cities and factories. There are lots of places where people have to work together. This is just a small town we got here. There's more room to spread out, and things move a little slower. Up until this whole civil rights thing got started a few years ago, things were pretty good here in town."

"Pretty good for everybody or just pretty good for white people?" I said.

The conversation between Lee and me was starting to get a little strained.

Bob picked up on the tension and said, "Let me tell you about this fellow that used to work down at the service station where your grandmother takes her car to get the oil changed and whatnot. Time was, you'd take the car in and this boy, Lewis

Tate is his name, Lewis would come out and fill the tank, wipe the windshield, check the oil, and smile big as you please the whole time. Sometimes people would tip him a dollar because he'd give such good service. Now, the last year or so, he changed. He got to be, well, kind of angry like."

I said, "This 'boy,' we're talking about, how old is he?"

"I don't know," Bob said. "He's got a couple kids pretty close to your age,"

"Well then he's not exactly a 'boy' then, is he?" I said.

"Well, I guess not, but you know that's just an expression. It don't mean nothing. Anyway, the last year or so, people got to noticing that Lewis didn't seem quite so friendly. Word was he even wrote a letter to Martin Luther King asking him to come down to Fairweather to lead a protest against discrimination. I know for a fact he's written letters to the newspapers in Oklahoma City and Tulsa, and I hear he's got lots of other colored folks riled up, too."

"What about?"

"Well, to come back to your question from before, they're unhappy about how the school system is operated, you know, with white kids going to one school and coloreds going to the other. So, he and some other people went to a school board meeting and they got told it wasn't that the schools were segregated, it was that white people mostly lived on one side of town and the colored lived on the other side. And then when Lewis wanted to rent a house on the white side of the district, he was informed there wasn't anything available, but that he could put his name on a waiting list in case something opened up."

"I'm sure that fixed everything right up," I said sarcastically.

"It might have," Bob continued, "except nothing ever did come available. But that didn't stop Lewis from complaining to everybody that came in to buy gas about how he thought his kids weren't getting a fair opportunity. Finally, Mr. Wilhelm, he's the man that owns the service station,

Mr. Wilhelm had to let Lewis go. Too many customers were starting to take their trade to another station. Now my daddy says Lewis has gone and hired himself a lawyer from the law school at the University of Oklahoma. He wants to sue Mr. Wilhelm and the school board for racial discrimination."

"And the town blames this man for all that?" I said.

"Well, yeah, in a way. I mean a lot of folks are kind of upset. If he'd just waited a while longer, chances are things would have worked themselves out on their own. As it is, you never can tell what might happen. We got a few hotheads in town, and I'd hate to think what they might do if things get pushed too far."

Lee, who had gone back to tinkering with the engine while Bob was talking, had finally had enough. He dropped his wrench in the dirt and looked up at me angrily. "What do you care about this, anyway? Ain't you got enough problems of your own back home that you need to come down here and tell us what we ought to be doin'?"

He had a point. Before I met Dr. Oswald, I would have said that, except for what I saw on television news, I hadn't paid much attention at all to whatever problems there were between whites and Negroes. Now my father was fighting for his life and a Negro doctor was his best hope for winning that fight. I had to think about questions that affected me very personally. Because of dad's situation, I had no choice but to hope, and even believe, that colored people really were just as capable as white people and deserved to be treated the same.

I was getting angry and I wanted to say something, but Bob cut me off. "Look Gary, I'm sure this is all going to work out fine for your dad and for this Lewis Tate fella here. Like Lee says, sometimes it takes a while for people to get their heads on straight. In the meantime, there ain't much any of us can do except wait and let things work themselves out on their own."

"Sounds like another way of saying nobody really gives a damn," I said, looking directly at Lee.

Lee crawled out from under the engine and stood up. His face had gone fiery and I thought he was going to challenge me to a fight.

"Look here. You don't know a thing about how it is here in Fairweather. Just because politicians are talking big in Washington or there are colored doctors in St. Louis, that don't mean any of that is going to happen here. So you can go along believing everything you read in some newspaper if you want to, but don't think that gives you the right to come down here and tell us how we ought to live our lives. We were just fine before you got here, and we'll be just fine after you're gone."

"Yeah, I guess," I said. "By the way, did either one of you look this engine over at all before you paid for it?"

"I did," Lee said. "And there ain't a thing wrong with it."

"Maybe not mechanically," I said, "except that it isn't a 409, it's a 348. A 409 has the tube for the oil dip stick on the passenger side. This engine here has the dipstick on the driver's side. That makes it a 348, and that means you're only going to get 280 horsepower, tops. A 409 will make 360 horses, and that might be what you paid for, but that's not what you got."

Bob and Lee looked at one another in disbelief.

"And just in case you're wondering, it was something I read in a magazine."

CHAPTER TEN:
A Golf Lesson

After my first weekend in Fairweather, life began to settle into a routine. Mornings Grandmother got up early to drive Granddad to work at the railroad depot. Then she came back home and made breakfast for Bob and me. About eight-thirty Lee came by and picked up Bob and drove them both to their summer job at the Ottawa County Park District where they did landscape chores in the city parks. Evenings, Bob and I would go downtown and cruise the drive-ins, or else Lee would come over and the three of us would work on getting the new engine installed in Bob's Chevy.

Bob had checked into what I had told him about the engine being a 348 and not a 409, and sure enough, I was right. Bob called Uncle Warren in Kansas City and Uncle Warren talked to the man who had sold him the engine in the first place. The man promised to send Bob a refund of seventy-five dollars. With that money Lee and Bob figured they could buy some new parts and get enough extra power out of the 348 so that it would make almost as much horsepower as a 409.

The nights we cruised the drive-ins, Bob made a beeline for Bonnie and I kept an eye out for Gideon. Since my first night in town, though, I had not seen him again. I thought about asking some of the other kids I had met whether they knew him, but the more time I spent around Bob's friends, the less likely it seemed to me that any of them would know Gideon. I had only met him once myself, but even in the short time we talked, he struck me as being very different from the kind of people Bob knew.

I was also starting to wonder about Bob's friends. Other than Lee and Rabbit, who lived right down the street from Grandmother's house, just about everyone else Bob hung around with lived on the north side of Fairweather. As I found out from Rabbit, that was where the families who had money lived. And even if I hadn't been told, it was obvious from the clothes they wore and the cars they drove that they were better off than the people who lived on our side of town. Lee had a '58 Ford. Bob was building a '51 Chevrolet with a hot motor. Rabbit had no car at all. Bob's friends, however, mostly had new cars, Mustangs and GTOs and even a few Corvettes. They weren't rescuing rides from the junkyard; they were buying them brand new at the dealership. It reminded me of the day Grandmother and Granddad took me to church with them. My grandparents didn't appear to have much money and yet they were perfectly comfortable socializing with people who did. I made up my mind that before I went back to St. Louis, this was a question I was going to get answered. In the meantime, my grandparents were keeping me busy.

Most days, after the breakfast dishes were done and before it got too hot, Grandmother set me to work in the yard and around the house. One day I painted the front porch railings. Other mornings, she had me pulling weeds in the garden patch or mowing the lawn; there always seemed to be something that needed to be done and to be honest, I was just as happy doing it. In the afternoons, after chores, I'd go outside and practice hitting golf balls, trying to keep my swing in shape. After a while, I got to be pretty consistent chipping balls into a three-foot circle I had marked in the grass with a loop of clothesline.

One day when Bob and Lee got home from work I was still out in the yard practicing. Usually the two of them headed straight for the garage to work on Bob's '51, but today Lee wandered over to see what I was doing.

"That don't look so hard," he said, after he'd watched me hit a few more. "Mind if I try?"

"Go ahead," I said. "Try to hit it into that circle over there."

So that he wouldn't knock a ball through a neighbor's window, I handed him a pitching wedge, which is a club designed to loft balls high into the air without traveling a great distance. I dropped a ball at his feet.

"Swing easy. Hit behind the ball a little bit

and just try to flip it up into the air."

"Okay," he said, "watch this."

He took a big swing and missed the ball completely. "That was just warming up." He took a second swing and missed again. On the third swing he made contact, but only barely, and shanked the ball sideways, knocking it into the door of his car where it struck with a loud "clunk."

"You're picking your head up," I said. "You're wanting to see where the ball is going before you actually hit it. If you did that playing baseball or even ping-pong the same thing would happen. You have to keep your eye on the ball."

"Yeah, well, I guess I'll stick with football and tearing engines apart, but hey, if you're interested, my sister Darby plays golf. If you want, I'll ask her if she wants to take you on."

He made it sound like a boxing match. "Is she any good?"

I looked over at Bob and he gave me a look that said something pretty close to "Be careful what you ask for," but I didn't care. After nearly a week of hanging around my grandparents' house every day, it would have been fine with me if she played with a rake and a shovel.

"Never saw her play, but I think she's fair."

"Sure," I said, "go ahead and ask her."

Lee and Bob spent the next hour fiddling with the engine before Grandmother called us in for supper.

After Lee had gone I said to Bob, "Tell me about, what's her name, Debby?"

"Not Debby, Darby, and there ain't much to tell. She keeps pretty much to herself and she ain't much on looks, but I do hear she plays a good game of golf. Other than that, I expect you'll just have to wait and find out for yourself."

A few minutes later Lee telephoned and said Darby had agreed to play. He said he'd drop us off at the park course in the morning and then run us back home at lunchtime. During supper I mentioned to Grandmother and Granddad that I had a golf date in the morning and asked to be excused from chores for the day.

Grandmother looked at me over the rims of her glasses. "You're planning on meeting up with Darby Lathrop?"

"Just to play golf," I said. "Why, is there some reason why I shouldn't?"

"Some folks think she's a mite odd," Granddad said. "Me, I believe it takes all kinds to make a world. I'm sure you'll get along just fine."

The next morning when Lee arrived to pick up Bob and me, his sister Darby was sitting in the passenger seat. At least I guessed it must be his sister. Bob had been right about one thing: she wasn't very good looking, and in fact, at first glance it wasn't even obvious whether she was a girl. She had on a gray sweatshirt, blue jeans, a dirty blue baseball cap and black high-top sneakers. Her straight hair was cut short and she wore no makeup. Lee opened his trunk and I stowed my golf clubs. There weren't any other clubs in the trunk, and I wondered what Darby was going to use to play with. Maybe she kept her set at the golf course.

Bob and I squeezed into the back seat. I

leaned forward and held out my hand to Darby. "Hi. I'm Gary, Bob's nephew."

"Darby," she said, shaking my hand.

"Lee says you play a pretty good game," I said.

"I do okay," she said.

"Do you know your handicap?" I asked. In golf, handicap is a way for players of different ability to compare with one another in tournaments. The lower a player's handicap, the better a player he or she is; the higher the handicap, the worse. The way it works is at the end of the round you subtract your handicap from your actual score. That gives you a net score, and the system is set up so that if both players shoot their average, the better player will still have a lower net score and win the match. In my case, I have a handicap of fifteen, meaning that I normally shoot around 90.

Darby said, "About ten, I think."

Ten! That meant she regularly shot in the low 80s. If we were playing in a tournament, she would have to give me five strokes, the difference between her handicap and mine. It also meant that if I shot my average and she shot hers, her net score would be two or three strokes lower than mine. She would win, and I would lose, *to a girl*.

When we got to the golf course, which was part of the city park, we paid our green fees and walked out to the first tee. There I got two more surprises. First, Darby had no clubs.

"I was hoping you wouldn't mind if I used yours," she said. "I've been saving up for a set, but then I loaned some of the money to Lee to buy that engine for his car. He's planning to race it and pay me back out of the money he wins."

"I guess that would be okay," I said. "You don't have any shoes either?"

"I'm wearing them," she said, pointing to the high tops she had on in the car. "Besides, I don't plan to hit the ball with my feet, which reminds me, I'm gonna need to borrow a ball if it's not too much trouble."

"Not a bit," I said, wondering what I had gotten myself into. I tossed her a ball from my bag.

"You want to go ahead and hit first?"

"Because ladies go first?" she said, giving me the first smile I'd seen. And that's when I got my second surprise.

The way golf courses are set up there are three sets of tee markers, each about five yards apart. The closest are the ladies' tees, then the men's tees and then what are called the blue tees, which are the farthest back, and which are used by professionals when they play in tournaments. I expected Darby would set up on the ladies' tee. Instead, she selected the driver from my bag, positioned herself at the men's tee, took one practice swing and then drilled the ball dead center down the fairway about two hundred yards.

I hit my own tee shot straight but swung under the ball just a little and popped it higher into the air than I wanted to. When it finally came down my ball bounced to a stop about twenty yards short of Darby's.

Because I was farthest from the green, I hit my second shot before she did. This time the ball bounced into a sand trap on the right side of the green. Darby's second shot landed on the front of the green. From there she needed two putts to sink the ball for a par. Meanwhile, it took me one more shot to get out of the sand, then three putts to finish.

After one hole I was already two shots down.

The rest of the front nine went pretty much the same way. Darby would hit her tee shot dead center in the fairway. Occasionally she would make a mistake and wind up in the sand, or three-putt a green, but she never did anything to get into real trouble. She just focused on her game, not paying any attention to me other than to stay close enough to select a club for her next shot.

Meanwhile, I was spraying the ball all over the place, and only a couple of miraculous recovery shots kept my score from being worse than it was. After nine holes and two lost balls I managed a 49. Darby, using my clubs and still the one ball I had given her, shot 40.

As we made the turn to head out on the back nine, I made up my mind that I was going to do whatever it took to win the match. It no longer mattered that Darby was a girl. I wasn't about to let anybody wearing tennis shoes and using my clubs beat me at the only game I was any good at. Maybe I couldn't hit a curve ball, but I could hit a golf ball, and I was going to beat Darby no matter what.

The tenth hole was a long one, 510 yards and a par 5. Darby hit her usual drive into the middle of the fairway about 210 yards out. I was determined that this time I would show her how I could really play the game. The wind was behind us and so I teed the ball up a little higher than usual, thinking I could catch a strong gust and maybe gain a few extra yards.

Grip it and rip it, as the pros say.

I swung as hard as I could, knowing that if I caught it right I could hit it 250 yards.

I hit it solidly, but unfortunately my timing was a little off. I felt it as soon as the club made contact. The ball took off to the left and rocketed out about 75 yards before it caught part of a tree limb and dropped straight to the ground. That was the final straw. All the frustration I had been feeling all morning, and for that matter, the past week, boiled over. I wound up and threw my club as far as I could into the middle of the fairway.

It was a really stupid thing to do. In the summertime and on weekends I had a job caddying at a country club near home and sometimes I would see players get angry and throw clubs after making a bad shot. Of course, since I was just a caddy I never said anything, but it always seemed to be very childish to me, especially since it was a game that was supposed to be fun.

I turned to face Darby, expecting her to laugh at me. When she didn't, still angry, I said, "I suck."

"No, but what you just did sucks. Look, do you mind if I give you some advice?"

"Go ahead," I said, not really wanting to hear it, but also not knowing what else I could say.

"Okay, you play pretty well, but you aren't going to beat me, not today or any other day if you keep doing what you're doing."

"You mean playing like crap."

"Well, yeah, but not for the reason you think. See, you already know this, but the thing about golf is that there isn't any defense. It's just you and the course, so if you get a hole in one on every single hole, there isn't anything I can do about it except keep playing my own game. I've been watching you for ten holes and the only thing I see you doing is worrying about what I'm doing. You're hoping that I'll hit a bad shot because that will take the pressure off you to make a good one.

"Anyhow, here's the reason you aren't going to beat me. I've been playing golf almost ten years. Because of that, right now, I'm a better player than you and that's all there is to it. So what you need to do is forget about me and start paying attention to your own game."

"I wanted to go out for the golf team next year," I said miserably.

"You should, and you'll probably make it," she said. "You're good enough as long as you keep your head on straight. Me, I'm hoping for a golf scholarship to Tulsa or Oklahoma State, so I can't screw around with this. If I don't get a scholarship, I'm not going to college, and if I don't go to college, I'll never get out of this town."

This was the second time I'd heard somebody say that. "You could join the Marines," I said.

"You mean like that idiot uncle of yours?" she said, and we both laughed. It was the first time I'd heard her laugh, and when she did her whole appearance changed. She didn't suddenly turn into a movie star, but she was a lot better looking than I had first thought.

"Has Bob told your grandmother about joining up yet?"

Because I wasn't sure how much she actually knew, I didn't answer right away.

"It's okay," she said. "Bob told Rabbit and Rabbit told Lee and, well, you know the rest. It's a small town."

"I'm pretty sure he hasn't," I said. "If he had I'm guessing everybody up and down the street would know it, too."

"Yeah, they'd figure something was up about the same time they saw the roof fly off the house," she said. "Listen, tell you what. I've had enough for one day, and to be honest, your clubs don't fit me that well. How about you finish your round and I'll just walk along and maybe give you a couple of pointers. That is, if you don't mind a little coaching."

"That'd be great," I said, and that's what we did. Darby had been right about one thing. Once I stopped watching to see what she was doing, my game began to come back together. Now and then she would offer a suggestion about adjusting my stance or positioning the club face, and by following her advice and concentrating on what I was doing I finished the back nine with a 42, and a

91 for the day. If I had played the front nine the same way I played the back, I would have had one of my best rounds ever. I guess that was the point she was trying to make.

When we got back to the clubhouse, Lee was waiting in his Ford to pick us up. "How'd it go?" he asked.

"Too good for me," Darby said. "I quit after ten."

Lee was on his lunch break so there was no time for us to stop anywhere on the way home to get something to eat. As I was getting my clubs out of the trunk, Darby leaned out the window and said, "Here, I forgot to give this back," and handed me the ball I had given her that morning.

I made up my mind right then that no matter what, that was one ball I would keep forever.

CHAPTER ELEVEN:
A Letter from Home

The next afternoon I got my first letters from home. Grandmother had left them on the table just inside the front door. I found them when I came in for lunch after mowing the side yard. One was from Mom and to my surprise, the other was from Wendy. I took them into the living room where I could be by myself. I sat on the couch trying to make up my mind which one to open first. I finally decided I'd start with Mom's.

Dear Gary,

I thought you might have written by now, but I guess maybe you are busy making new friends and getting caught up with what has been going on with Grandmother, Granddad and your Uncle Bob. Please tell them I know they must be terribly worried and that I owe them a telephone call and will be in touch in the next day or two.

As you might imagine, I have been very busy here, what with work and spending most of the rest of my time at the hospital. I wish I could tell you that Dad is getting better, and maybe he is, but if so, I haven't seen any sign of it. Of course, it has only been about ten days, so Doctor Oswald is still hopeful. One of the nurses told me he said a few words the night you left for Fairweather. At first, we thought that was a good sign, but he hasn't said anything more since then, so nobody knows whether that was a step forward or just something that happened. In the meantime, all we can do is hope and pray.

Well, that's about it for now. I have to get ready for work and I will drop this in the mailbox on my way. Oh, Pete's cousin Wendy called right after you left. She said she was sorry she missed your call. I gave her your grandmother's address so you might be getting a note from her one of these days. Please write soon and let me know how you are getting along. I miss you very much and hope that next time I write I will be able to give you better news.

Love,

Mom

PS: I am enclosing $20 to keep you going for a while longer. Maybe you could treat Grandmother and Granddad to dinner some night. Be sure to give them both my love.

Next, I opened the letter from Wendy. It was written on light blue stationery that smelled like flowers. It read:

Dear Gary,

I was very sorry to hear what happened to your dad, and also sorry I missed your call the night before you left for your grandparents' house in Oklahoma. I know now I should have called you back when I got home from studying, but it was a little late and I thought I'd see you the next day at school.

We had a really great graduation ceremony. Phil read the valedictory speech and (don't _ever_ tell him I said this) he did a very good job. He even mentioned you. He said something like,

"Graduation is a time for looking ahead as well as looking back. And as we look back we should remember our friend Gary Seiler who cannot be here tonight because of an illness in his family," and when he said that, everybody applauded. You have more friends than you know about, and you should feel good about that.

Phil also said that you had talked to him about me. I know this is probably not the right time to bring this up, but I do like you a lot, Gary, and if what Phil says is right, I guess maybe you like me, too. I hope when you get back that you will call me again, so we can talk and maybe spend some time together. Also, if you're not terribly busy, possibly you could write to me and let me know how things are going for you in Oklahoma. I know it must be hard being away from home.

Anyway, I wanted you to know I was thinking about you and hope that everything is okay.

Love,

Wendy

As I was finishing reading each of the letters for the second time, Grandmother came into the room and sat down.

"I see you got a letter from your mom. I ain't wanting to be nosy, but I am wondering if she said anything about whether your dad is doing any better. I expect I should have telephoned her before this, but to tell the truth I can't help thinking no news is good news."

I handed her the letter I had received from Mom. "I think in this case no news is just that. It doesn't sound like there's been any change at all."

Grandmother read Mom's letter and then handed it back to me. "Lord Almighty, this is hard," she said at last. "Your granddad and I were blessed with five sons. The war took your Uncle Ellis, and that was God's will and a righteous cause, but I never expected I might outlive any of my other boys, least of all Gideon. You know, it ain't right at all for a mother to have to bury any of her children. It's supposed to be the other way around." Her voice caught, and a tear ran down her cheek.

I started to tell her that I had met someone else named Gideon a couple of nights earlier, but decided now wasn't the time. "Grandmother, I'm sure Dad will be fine. He's in a good hospital and they're taking good care of him."

"I know," she said. "And I know I shouldn't carry on like this, least of all in front of you. It's me that should be telling you everything will be all right."

"It's okay, Grandmother. We can keep telling one another."

We sat quietly for a little while after that, listening to the sound of the big wind-up clock ticking from its perch on top of the fireplace mantel. Hanging on the wall opposite where I was sitting was a photograph of Dad and my three oldest uncles, taken just before Dad joined the Navy in the summer of 1944, and before Bob was born a few years later.

Uncle Ellis, the oldest of the four brothers, was wearing his Army Air Force uniform. I remembered being told he had piloted a B-24 bomber flying daylight missions over Germany. His plane had been hit by anti-aircraft fire during a run in early 1945. His Liberator crashed, and his body was never recovered. He held the rank of major and in the photo he looked as proud and brave as a star in a Hollywood picture.

Uncle Warren was the next oldest. There was something the matter with his heart, so he never got drafted and he wasn't allowed to enlist, either. Eventually he got a job with a printing company and moved to Kansas City. Uncle Ronald did get drafted in 1943 and served in the Army in North Africa and Sicily before getting wounded in Italy at a place called Anzio. He was shipped back home and spent several months in a military hospital in Baltimore. After he recovered from his wounds he was assigned to a training battalion at Fort Polk,

Louisiana. When the war was over he came back to Fairweather, married Aunt Virginia and has lived there ever since.

Dad was the youngest of the four. Instead of waiting to get drafted, he joined the Navy in late 1944. He went through basic training in California and was on a ship heading toward Japan when the war ended the following August. The ship turned around and came back to San Francisco, so World War II ended without Dad ever actually being involved in the fighting.

With four grown sons, it must have been quite a surprise for Grandmother and Granddad when Bob came along in 1947. Dad used to say there were a lot of jokes at family get-togethers about that.

"Grandmother," I said at last, "can I ask you a question?"

"Long as it ain't about girls." She smiled and nodded in the direction of the two envelopes lying next to me on the arm of the chair. "I saw you got two letters."

"No, it's not about that. I was wondering," I stopped, not sure about the right words to use, "I was wondering why you don't like Mom."

She seemed surprised at the question. "Why would you think a thing like that?"

"Because that's what Mom thinks. I just want to understand what that's all about, because I have a feeling we're all going to need one another's help before too much longer. We can't do that if we can't get along."

"Your mother and dad raised you up pretty smart, I can tell," she said.

"Not so smart. If they had, maybe I'd understand some of this stuff better."

Grandmother looked at me for a long time before she spoke. "After your dad got out of high school, we all knew it was just a matter of time before he got drafted. And of course, with the war still going on, it was a sure thing that he was going to be shipped overseas." She sighed, as if the memory were a painful one. "That's probably what's going to happen with Bob after he graduates, because I surely don't see him going to college. I expect the Army will call him up and send him off to Vietnam.

"Anyway, before his draft notice came your dad went down and joined the Navy, which was all well and good since we thought that might be safer on board a ship than coming ashore with the Marines on some island where the Japanese were dug in. Well, he no sooner shipped out than the war ended and we all breathed a sigh of relief that we were going to get him back in one piece. You already know that part, I guess."

I nodded. "Dad always says he was lucky."

"As far as the coming home safe, he was. He did his duty for his country and nobody could say he didn't.

"After he got discharged, your dad wasn't back in Fairweather more than a week when he announced he and your mom were getting married and moving to St. Louis. It seems he'd gotten a job with the Frisco. Now he and your mom had been seeing one another right along through high school, so Granddad and I figured they'd be getting married some day. We hoped they'd settle down here in Fairweather where they'd be close. But your dad had other ideas about his future, and said so in no uncertain terms, and then words were said and your mom and I got into it and, well, that's pretty much the way things still stand."

"That's it?" I said. "The two of you got into an argument over Mom and Dad moving to St. Louis in 1945? Excuse me for saying this, but that's stupid."

"Like I said, words were spoken. Your mom and I called each other some pretty awful names and that's where things still more or less stand."

"I thought it might have something to do with Dad's drinking. I thought maybe you were blaming Mom for that."

"So he hasn't quit, then," she said. It wasn't a question.

"No, Grandmother, he hasn't," I said, remembering I had told her just the opposite the night I arrived. "And nobody has come out and said it, but I'm pretty sure he was drunk when he wrecked his car. I know I should have told you that the other night, but I just didn't think it was something you and Granddad wanted to hear right then. I'm sorry. I didn't come down here intending to lie to you."

"Don't be sorry. You only did what your heart told you was right. There ain't any sin in that. And anyway, your dad's drinking is his own problem, not anything anybody did to him. And it more or less goes back to the reason he didn't want to stay in Fairweather."

"I don't understand," I said.

"Your dad had big plans for his life, Gary. Move to the city, go to work for the railroad, finish college, wind up some kind of big executive and have a nice life. That was something he figured he couldn't do if he stayed here in a small town like this.

"But then he got to the city and things didn't quite work out the way he'd planned. Getting a college degree at night school took longer than he thought, and then you came along and, well, he was just disappointed with his life. I expect he took to drinking to take his mind off all the things he never did become. Unfortunately, climbing out of the bottle is a sight harder than falling in."

"If I live to be a hundred," I said, "I am never going to take a drink of liquor."

"It's good to hear you say that, Gary," Grandmother said. "But you might find it's a hard promise to keep."

After that there didn't seem to be anything else to talk about, and once again the clock ticking on the mantel was the only sound.

Finally, Grandmother said, "I expect when your dad is better, your mom and I should get together and put things right. You know, Gary, life is too short to waste the longest part of it with anger in your heart over things that could be fixed with a simple apology and a few words of kindness."

Grandmother shook her head sadly. Then she got up from her chair and went into the kitchen to begin making supper.

CHAPTER TWELVE:
Off to the Races

It took another couple of days before I got around to answering the letters I got from Mom and Wendy. I'm not very good at writing letters, especially when it comes to talking about feelings.

Answering Mom wouldn't be too hard, I knew. She just wanted to be sure that I was doing okay so she wouldn't have one more thing to worry about, and I knew that by not writing I was probably giving her exactly that. And although she could have picked up the phone any time and just called, I figured she hadn't because she was afraid Grandmother might answer and then she wouldn't know what to say.

So finally, on a morning when there were no chores for me to do and it was already too hot to do anything else outside, I picked up a pen and paper and began to write.

Dear Mom,

I got your letter two days ago. Thanks for sending the extra money. I'm not sure when I'm going to have the chance to spend it, though. Pretty much all we do is go into town at night and hang around the A&W Root Beer stand. This gives Bob the chance to see his girlfriend, who he can't just ask out on a date because her father doesn't like him.

If you decide to call please don't tell Grandmother, but Bob has joined the Marines! They're going to take him as soon as he turns 18 which is in a couple of months. That means he's going to drop out of high school. He says it's the only way he can get out of Fairweather and do something with his life. It's funny, but Grandmother says that's the same idea Dad had when he went to work for the Frisco and moved to St. Louis. You know, you might want to give Grandmother a call some time and talk things over. I'm pretty sure she's gotten over whatever it was that you two argued about back when you and Dad got married.

I've met a few people, but I haven't really made any friends. There are these guys Lee and Rabbit who live down the street. Lee is helping Bob put an engine into this old car he's fixing up. The two of them drove up to Kansas City to buy an engine Uncle Warren found in a junk yard. They thought they were buying a 409 but it turned out to be a 348, which isn't nearly as good. If they had taken me along, I could have told them they had the wrong engine, but they didn't, so now Bob is stuck. I also met Lee's sister. Her name is Darby. She's a few years older than me and she plays golf. So far we've played once and she beat me pretty good. I was embarrassed at the time, but now I think I can learn from her, so I hope we will have the chance to play again.

Your letter didn't sound like Dad is getting any better. I hope that changes soon, because I really want to come home. I don't fit in down here and I really don't understand how some things work. Bob was telling me about a colored man named Lewis Tate who lost his job for trying to get his daughter into a white school and now we heard that he has disappeared. Nobody seems to know where he went, but they don't think he moved out because his family is still here and they don't know where he went either.

I don't really have anything else to tell you except that tonight Bob, Lee, Rabbit and I are going to a stock car race at the county fairgrounds. I'm kind of excited about it because if nothing else it

means I won't be stuck another night at the A&W.
Please write soon and tell me Dad is getting better.
I miss being home and want to see everybody
before summer is over.

Love,

Gary

Answering Wendy's letter was more complicated. Of course, I was absolutely thrilled that she wanted to see me, and I had already started daydreaming about what that small wish might lead to. I just didn't know what to say back to her that would sound right without making me seem like an idiot. I remembered what a hard time I'd had just trying to figure out what to say to her on the phone. What was I going to put into a letter that she would be able to read over and over again, or, worse yet, show to her friends?

Well, what the hell, I thought. I'd never know until I tried and if I didn't like it I could always tear it up and start over again. In fact, that's exactly what happened. It took me three tries, but this is what I finally wrote:

Dear Wendy,

Thanks very much for your letter. I wish I could have been there for graduation. I know it's just a ceremony and that it doesn't mean very much, but it would have been cool to be with everybody and to hear Phil's speech (of course then he wouldn't have mentioned my name).

I got a letter from my mom the same day yours came. My dad isn't doing any better, and we're getting very worried he might not. Even Grandmother, who is a very strong woman, doesn't talk about it much, although I'm sure she thinks about it all the time. I hope he starts getting well soon, not only because it will be really hard for Mom if he doesn't, but also because I want to come home. The people here are okay, I guess, but they have some funny ideas about certain things and I think no matter how long I stay here I'm never going to fit in.

Wendy, this is the third time I have tried to write this part of this letter, and I still can't think of a good way to say what I want to say, so I'm just going to come right out and say it (does that even make any sense?). I like you a lot, too. I have for a long time, and when I read in your letter that you liked me it was like getting a very special present when it isn't even my birthday. I have read what you wrote over and over again, and the only thing I can say is that I hope you weren't just writing that to cheer me up. I have never had a girlfriend or even known a girl I would want for a girlfriend before now and I can't wait to get home so we can get to know each other better. I hope this doesn't sound too stupid, but if I don't just say this now, I'm afraid I never will. Please write again soon

Boy, who was I kidding? I'd never even been out on a date before, let alone had a girlfriend. Closing that letter "love" felt like the biggest risk I had ever taken in my life. And then I took an even bigger one. I put the letter in an envelope, put a stamp on it, walked it down to the corner and dropped it in the mailbox.

    *   *   *   *

I had it in my head that the race track at the fairgrounds was going to look something like the Indianapolis Motor Speedway where the 500 Mile Race is held every Memorial Day. Of course, I have never actually been to Indianapolis, but I watch the race on television every year, and I know it's an oval, 2½ miles long, with space in the middle big

enough for a golf course and a museum to fit inside.
By comparison, the track at the Neosho County
fairgrounds wasn't much bigger than the track
behind our school. Unlike the track at Indianapolis,
this one was flat rather than banked and the surface
was hard-packed clay rather than concrete or
blacktop. However, the air was filled with the
smells of gasoline and popcorn and hotdogs grilling,
and the sounds of engines revving through their
final tune-ups. So although it wasn't Indianapolis, it
felt like it was going to be a fun night.

"This is dirt track racing, but most folks call
it roundy-round," Rabbit explained as we settled
into our seats, which were just like the bleachers at
school. "The track is three-eighths of a mile, so the
cars bunch up a lot, especially in the turns. That's
most often when you see crashes."

"How many cars are on the track at one
time?" I asked. I was thinking about the Indy 500,
which starts with a field of 33 cars.

Lee said, "Generally there are ten or twelve.
There ain't room for any more on a small track like

this. Plus, the races are mostly short, ten laps or so. The feature race, that'll be the last one, that's 25 laps. But the thing is, the track is so small that once somebody breaks out in front, nobody has the room to pass him unless he crashes or his car quits running."

I looked around to get a sense of what we were going to be watching. We were sitting in a grandstand that ran the length of the front straightaway. More seats curved partway around the first and last turns. There was a low concrete wall topped by a chain link fence that separated the track from the seating area. Rabbit assured me the wall was strong enough to stop a car from crashing into the stands and the fence would catch any parts that might come flying off the cars. Dirt from the track, however, was a different story. It could and did come through the fence whenever one of the cars lost traction and spun its wheels, which happened a lot.

The race cars were also not like anything I had seen before. They had bodies made from steel tubes welded together to form an open cage where the driver sat. There were no fenders, no doors and only a single seat for the driver. Flat pieces of steel were fastened to the sides of the cars to partially enclose the drivers, whose safety equipment consisted of a helmet and a three-point harness to protect them in case of a crash. I asked Bob what kind of engines they were running.

"Small-block Chevy's, mostly," he said. "A few run Fords, but the Chevies are easier to get parts for, and they rev up quick. See these here cars don't have transmissions like what you might think about. They've got one gear and a clutch, but no shifter, so you're either in gear or you're out. On a short track like this one there's no time to shift anyway. Just watch. You'll get the hang of it pretty soon."

I couldn't say for sure how many people were in the stands, but I guessed three hundred. Most of them were sitting up about halfway up in the stands, and as soon as the first race started I understood why. Bob, Rabbit, Lee and I were seated about ten rows back from the barrier wall and right at the end of the fourth turn where the cars accelerated as they entered the front straightaway and headed toward the finish line. If you were a real race fan this was a perfect spot, because you got all the noise, dirt and smell of unburned racing fuel. If you were not, you just got filthy.

The first race was ten laps with only seven cars entered. As Lee had predicted, a car with the number "89" jumped out in front on the second lap and held the lead until the end. It turned out the prize for winning was $100. The crowd cheered as Car 89 took a victory lap, and it was plain that a lot of the people in the stands knew the drivers and were rooting for their favorites.

The rest of the races all went the same way. One car would grab the lead and hold on while the rest of the cars tried with only occasional success to catch up and pass.

About halfway through the fourth race, two cars ran into each other coming out of the second turn and both of them ended up spinning out of control into the infield. Nobody was hurt and neither of the cars flipped over, but both of them were too badly damaged to get back on the track.

As they spun out, dirt flew everywhere, and the crowd stood up to get a better look. It was plain that spin-outs and crashes were what a lot of people had come to see, and to be honest they were more exciting than just watching the cars going around the track. Seeing them circling over and over like a Lionel train under a Christmas tree made it obvious how roundy-round racing got its name.

After a while I started to get dizzy watching the cars through the fence.

"I'm going to move up a little higher for the last race," I told Bob, but I wasn't sure he heard me. He and Lee were deep into a discussion about whether Bob's '51 Chevy was going to need a stronger rear axle now that the 348 was making more horsepower.

I went to the far end of the stands, just beyond the first turn, and settled into a spot near the top row. Nobody else was sitting close to me, and perched up high the way I was, I could see over the top of the fence and get a clearer view of the cars coming down the front straightaway.

There was an intermission between the races, and with no cars running and the track announcer not talking, things became momentarily quiet.

I leaned back against the row of seats behind me and looked up at the sky, thinking I might be able to see the stars. I had the goofy idea that if Wendy was out in her back yard at that moment, she would be looking up at the same stars that were winking down at me.

That struck me as romantic.

However, with the stadium lights lit the only thing I could see were insects buzzing around in the glare, a sight that was definitely not romantic.

On the seat next to me somebody had carved the initials "JS + DB" with a heart around them. I traced the outline of the heart with my finger. That started me thinking about Wendy again, and Mom and Dad, and home. And more than anything, home was where I wanted to be.

"Enjoying the race?" A voice coming from behind me brought me out of my daydream and back into the moment. I turned, and there was Gideon with a wide grin on his face. "Haven't seen you for a while," he said, extending his hand for me to shake. "I thought maybe you'd already gone back to St. Louis."

"Not yet," I said, taking his hand. "And from the look of things it might not be for a while yet."

"You talked to your mother." He didn't say it like a question, and for some reason I got the feeling he already knew the story.

"Got a letter," I said. "It just came today."

"Have you heard from your girl?"

"You mean Wendy?" I hesitated, trying to remember whether I had mentioned Wendy when I had met Gideon the first time. I decided I must have, because otherwise how would he know about her?

"Yes. She sent a letter the same day Mom did. She said she'd like to see me when I get back."

"Well, that ought to give you something to look forward to, anyway," Gideon said. "Hey look, the feature race is about to start. Why don't we move closer to the starting line so we can get a better view?"

"I like it up here," I said. "It's easier to watch the cars without the fence in the way. Plus, I can see the whole track."

"Okay," he said. "Mind if I sit here with you?"

"No, not at all," I said. "Make yourself comfortable."

In another minute we heard the sound of engines starting and then cars began moving out onto the track to take their practice laps. Since none of the cars had mufflers, they made a lot of noise as they went around the track while the drivers got the feel of how their cars were going to perform once the race started.

After the cars had made a couple of laps the starter waved a checkered flag, indicating that the warmups were over, and the cars should take their positions at the starting line. The track announcer explained that the feature race was going to be 25 laps and that the winner would receive five hundred dollars, with three hundred going to the second-place car and two hundred to the third-place finisher. Any driver still running at the end of the race would be awarded fifty dollars.

"So, what have you been doing since I saw you last time," Gideon asked, "anything special?"

"I wouldn't call it that," I said. And I told him about how, other than playing one round of golf with Darby, I hadn't been doing anything much more exciting that hanging around with Bob in the evening and taking care of my grandparents' yard during the day.

"Well, maybe it helps keep your mind off why you're here in the first place," Gideon said. "Come on; let's go get something to eat."

"Okay, but let's wait until the race starts. The first couple of laps are all that's really interesting anyway."

The cars got into position at the starting line, and as the drivers were revving their engines, the starter waved his checkered flag again and the race began.

Dirt went flying into the air and the crowd noise swelled immediately as drivers began to maneuver for position. The first two times around the track the cars were all bunched up, with nobody able to break free of the pack. About halfway through the third lap three cars began to pull ahead. One of them was the same Number 89 which had won the first race. The two other leaders had run earlier that evening, but neither of them had won their previous races. I mentioned this to Gideon.

"The last race is just for the drivers that finished first or second in the qualifying heats. That makes the earlier races kind of like a playoff with the best two from each facing off in the feature. You ready to go get a hot dog or something?"

By this time, we were shouting to be heard over the noise coming from the track. "I'm not hungry," I said. "I want to see how this race turns out."

At that moment the strangest thing happened. Gideon reached over and grabbed my arm and as he did, all the noise from the crowd, from the track, from the announcer, from the cars on the highway beyond the fence suddenly dropped away. It was as if someone had disconnected the soundtrack from a movie playing in a crowded theater. Everything was still moving, but nothing was making a sound.

Startled, I looked at Gideon.

And then, even more strangely, he squeezed my left arm and said in a low voice that I could hear with perfect clarity, "Gary, we've got to move right now. Something bad is going to happen. We shouldn't be sitting here."

The look in his eyes stopped me from arguing. I heard myself say, "Okay, then let's go."

We started back down the steps toward the

exit ramp. At the exact moment I turned to ask him what was so important that we had to move, the noise that had melted away seconds earlier suddenly returned at full volume. In quick succession I heard the crowd let out what sounded like a collective gasp, followed a split second later by the screech of grinding metal and then a "WHUMP" that came from the track.

I turned in time to see two of the lead cars spin into the concrete retaining wall and then flip end over end, one car coming down on top of the other. As the first car hit the dirt, the front wheel and part of the axle sheared completely off and went flying into the air. As I watched, wheel, tire and axle soared in an impossibly high arc over the wire fence and landed in the grandstand in exactly the spot where Gideon and I had been sitting a moment before. The impact had enough force to tear a three-foot section out of the bleacher seats and then bounce two more times before coming to rest against the railing at the top of the stands.

"What the hell?" It took me a moment to realize what had happened. Then I turned to Gideon. "Did you see that? That thing landed right where we just were a minute ago! We would have been killed!"

The race crawled along under a yellow flag while the drivers of the two wrecked cars pulled themselves free of the wreckage. I barely noticed that, though. My attention was fixed on the spot where the seats had been wiped out and where, except for a lucky twist of fate, we would have been wiped out with it.

And then another thought came to me.

"You knew! That's why you wanted me to leave with you." I was screaming at Gideon, and I didn't care who heard me. "You knew that was going to happen!"

By this time people were starting to move in our direction, anxious to see what had happened and to find out whether anyone had been hurt. I picked Bob's face out of the crowd and waved to him to let him know I was okay. I turned back to Gideon to demand that he explain how he had chosen that exact moment to insist we move, but he was gone! He must have slipped down the stairway to the lower level of the stands, because one moment he was there and the next he was nowhere in sight.

Bob pushed his way through the crowd to where I was standing. Lee and Rabbit were right behind him.

"Are you okay?" he asked breathlessly. "When I saw that thing go flying I thought you were a goner for sure!"

"I would have been if Gideon hadn't made me move."

Bob looked at me, puzzled. "Who's Gideon?"

"He's a guy I met at the A&W my first night in town. I don't know his last name, but he says he knows you. He was just here. Didn't you see him?"

Bob looked first at Lee, then Rabbit, and then shook his head. "Except for your dad, I don't know anybody named Gideon. And when I looked up here just a minute ago, there wasn't anybody sitting up there besides you."

CHAPTER THIRTEEN:
Darby

That night I lay awake in bed thinking about what had happened at the race, and about Gideon. Either through a stroke of unbelievable luck or by somehow being able to see through a window into the future, he had saved my life. If he had not insisted that we move to another spot at the exact moment he did, right now I would be dead.

No matter how often I went over it in my mind, I couldn't understand how Bob, Lee and Rabbit had each failed to notice Gideon after the accident, especially since he had been standing right there with me. At the same time, they all agreed that they were actually looking to see if I was okay, so they weren't paying attention to anybody else. In other words, they couldn't say for sure if he had been there or not. As I stared into the darkness I began to wonder whether it was possible I had simply imagined the entire conversation with Gideon. But how could that be? I certainly hadn't imagined that tire flying into the stands and I hadn't imagined Gideon insisting we move out of the way seconds before it came crashing down. That much was real.

Grandmother and Granddad were in bed by the time Bob and I got home, but when they heard the story the next morning at breakfast Grandmother got pretty upset. She said that with Dad sick it would be a downright shame for me to come all the way to Fairweather just to get myself killed, and that Bob should have known better than to take me to something as dangerous as a stock car race. Bob tried to point out that it wasn't our fault there was a crash and anyway, nobody had gotten hurt, but Grandmother wasn't having any of that. She said that as long as she was responsible for keeping me in one piece there wouldn't be any more car races and that was all there was to it.

Granddad was a lot cooler. He said accidents happen, and since nobody but me had actually seen him, maybe Gideon was some kind of guardian angel who was looking after me while Dad was in the hospital.

That sent the conversation off in a completely different direction.

Grandmother said there was no way Gideon could be an angel because according to the Bible, the real Gideon was not an angel but an actual person who led the Israelites into battle back in the days of the Old Testament.

Then Bob made the mistake of speaking up and saying what difference did it make? Everybody knows the Bible is just a collection of stories made up to explain the causes of things like eclipses and swarms of grasshoppers that happened for reasons nobody at the time could figure out.

That comment made Grandmother's face turn red, but luckily for Bob, Granddad said it was time for him to get to work and that we'd have to continue this later. The one thing Grandmother, Granddad and Bob did agree on was that none of them knew anybody in Fairweather named Gideon.

Later that morning, after Lee picked up Bob for work and Grandmother had gone to her monthly Eastern Star meeting, the telephone rang.

I hesitated to pick it up, afraid that it might be Mom with bad news. But then I decided that it was probably for Grandmother, and she would want me to take a message.

It wasn't for Grandmother, though. It was Darby, calling for me.

"Hey, my mom's not using the car today. You feel like giving me a rematch?"

I knew I needed the practice if I was to have any hope of making the golf team in the fall. But I also remembered how badly she had beaten me the last time, and how hard that was to take. Darby heard the hesitation in my voice.

"I'll make a deal with you," she said. "We won't keep score this time; we'll just knock the ball around. But that means no more bad temper from you, okay?"

"Okay," I said.

"Good. I'll be there in half an hour. And don't sweat the sticks. I've got my own."

As it turned out, she had more than sticks. When she showed up driving her mom's station wagon, she not only had clubs, she also had a completely different look. She wore plaid Bermuda shorts, a yellow golf shirt, a visor and sunglasses and, when we got to the course, white golf shoes with black saddle trim. She looked every inch like the professional women golfers I saw when flipping through *Sports Illustrated* in the school library.

It was too much. I couldn't just ignore it, and I was sure she was waiting for me to say something.

"You look great," was what I finally came up with. "Did Lee pay you back the money he borrowed to buy his engine?"

"You're asking because?" she said, enjoying my surprise.

"I guess because if I didn't know it was you, I wouldn't know it was you. I mean, I thought you didn't have clubs, let alone shoes."

"Oh, last time was just for effect," she said. "I always do that the first time I play with guys. I didn't want you to get the idea we were on a blind date. Plus, I figure if I look crappy like that right off, you'll think you should be able to beat poor little me. When it turns out I'm not that easy, you get all psyched out and start pressing. Then you wind up beating yourself, which is exactly what happened."

She smiled, and I had to admit she had figured me exactly right.

"Sorry if that pissed you off," she said. "But you should have guessed I had something better to wear if I was on the team at school. Come on, you ready to play some golf?"

We warmed up by splitting a bucket of balls on the practice range. Once we were on the first tee Darby started off the same way as last time. She hit from the men's tee and drove the ball about 200 yards into the center of the fairway. However, I remembered my previous lesson, and concentrated on my own game and not hers. I caught the ball right on the screws and drove my tee shot about 25 yards past her, also right down the middle.

"Much better," she said, and we started walking.

I hooked my second shot into the rough, but recovered with my third and two-putted for a bogey, one stroke better than the week before. Sure enough, we didn't take a score card, but I kept track of what I was doing just the same. I managed a par on the second hole, then par, par, bogey and bogey through six. On the seventh hole, a 175-yard par 3, I knocked a four wood to within a couple of feet of the flag and then holed it for a birdie. One more par and another bogey left me with a 39 for the front nine, ten shots better than last time.

"Still think you suck?" Darby asked.

"Not today. You just saw me play the best front nine of my life," I said.

"Thirty-nine, right?" Darby said, and she winked at me.

"You were keeping score?"

"I don't need a scorecard to count strokes. And just in case you're wondering, we tied. That was a good nine all the way around. What do you say; I'll buy lunch."

We had hot dogs and Cokes in the shade of a big cottonwood tree outside the clubhouse. The day was turning hot, but there was a light breeze that stirred the air just enough to keep it from being really uncomfortable. I was still feeling pretty good about my personal-best front nine, and without thinking it all the way through, I said, "So, is this a date?"

"Excuse me?" Darby put her Coke down and gave me a look that said I had just made a huge mistake.

"Well," I began. I instantly understood that I had about as much chance of talking my way out of this without totally embarrassing myself as I would have winning the U.S. Open. I could feel my neck and cheeks reddening. I needed to think of something to say, fast. What I came up with was hopelessly lame.

"I was just thinking about how you said you dressed the way you did last time because you didn't want me to think it was a date."

"Got you," she nodded knowingly. "You thought that since I dressed a little better and that I called you that maybe this time it was a date?"

"I guess so," I said, wishing the cottonwood tree would fall down and put an end to my embarrassment.

I wanted to say something more, like *I was just kidding*. But it was already too late for that, and anything else I could say would only make things worse. So I just kept my mouth shut and waited for the next words out of her mouth to crush me like a bug on a windshield. But instead, her look softened and she smiled.

"Look, I think you're really sweet. I do. I mean, I can't remember the last time I was on a date with a guy, but no, that's not what this is."

"I understand," I said.

"No, you don't," she said, "so I'll try to explain. The fact is…." She hesitated for just a moment. "The fact is, and I've never come out and said this to anybody, I really am not much into boys, if you take my meaning. And even if I were, we live about three hundred miles apart, so how would that work out once you go back home?

"The reason I called you this morning is that you are one of the few people I've met who is willing to come out here with me and who can actually give me a game. That makes you much more important than some jerk who just wants to take me to a drive-in movie because he thinks I might make out with him during the second feature. Unlike those guys, you and I actually have something in common, and that makes us friends." She sighed. "I don't have a whole lot of friends, you know what I mean?"

"Yes," I said, and I meant it, because in this town I didn't either.

"Okay, then. Let's go finish this game."

The back nine didn't turn out quite as well as the front, at least not for me. I got into trouble on the eleventh when my tee shot went into some trees and it took me a couple of shots to get out. I scuffled some more on the middle three holes and then on the seventeenth, what should have been an easy par four turned into a six when I hooked my drive into a pond on the left side of the fairway. Still, I finished with a 44 on the back and an 83 for the round. Darby beat me again with another 39 and a 78 for the day. And she was still hitting from the men's tees.

"Wow, this was a great day," she said as we loaded our clubs back into the station wagon. "I really enjoyed it. We'll have to do this again."

"I'd like that," I said. But as things turned out, we never got the chance.

CHAPTER FOURTEEN:
A Social Error

The next Friday afternoon Bob got home from work a little before his usual quitting time. Grandmother was cutting up a chicken she was planning to fry for supper. I was busy with a pile of potatoes she had put me to work peeling.

"There's a party at Rhonda Rutherford's house tonight, Mom," he told Grandmother as he came bouncing into the kitchen. "Mr. Willis let me off half an hour early so I could get ready."

"Well, you sure sound excited," Grandmother said. "This must be quite a hoedown."

Bob picked out an apple from a bowl on the table and took a bite. "I guess I am excited.

Everybody's going to be there, and you know any time the Rutherford's do anything it's always special." He turned to me with a look of mock regret. "Sorry I got to leave you home tonight, but this deal is by invite only."

"Yeah, I know," I told him. "I got mine about a week ago." I pulled a small envelope out of my back pocket and held it up for him to see.

"What?" Bob grabbed the invitation out of my hand and stared at it in disbelief. "Now how in the hell did you get that?"

Grandmother's head snapped around. "No need for you to foul the air with your vile language, Bob. If you can't keep your mouth clean you're not so big I can't wash it out for you."

I said, "Rhonda gave it to me one night last week when we were hanging out at Skelley's and you took off with Lee and Rabbit. I was sitting there by myself waiting for you guys to get back and Rhonda came over and asked me how I was enjoying spending my summer with you."

"What'd you tell her?"

I shrugged. "I told her it was okay, but it was a little hard getting around since I didn't have a driver's license and since you had to work most days. I said that other than playing golf with Darby and nights when we hang around at the drive-in, I really haven't had much chance to do anything.

"So, she said, 'Well then, I've got just the thing for you.' She told me she was having a party at her house and that I should be sure to be there. She said if I couldn't get a lift to just call her and she'd have somebody come and pick me up. She even wrote her telephone number on the back of the card."

Bob took another bite of his apple. "Don't know why she'd think that'd be a problem. She knows you'll be riding with me."

"Well maybe she just wanted to make sure I'd be there, you know, in case you had something better to do."

"Did she say anything about who else was coming?"

"No, she didn't, and I didn't think to ask. It wouldn't have made any difference if she'd told me since I only know about three people besides you. Anyway, that was about it. I thanked her and told her I'd try and be sure to be there and she said she was looking forward to it and went off to talk to some of her friends."

*   *   *   *

Grandmother had supper ready early to give Bob and me time to shower and get ready for the party. I was feeling pretty good about myself. I had somehow managed to get invited to what was shaping up as a major social event, and had even been personally invited by the most popular girl in town. I therefore took care to make sure I looked my best.

I took an extra-long shower and, even though I didn't have to shave, splashed on some Old Spice I found in the medicine cabinet. I put on a pair of white Levis, a plaid short-sleeved shirt and even buffed up my penny loafers so they were shiny. I borrowed some of Bill's tonic and slicked my hair back, so I looked the way Dick Clark looked on *American Bandstand*.

I checked myself in the mirror and practiced my smile. I was ready to rock and roll. I was all set to show these small-town bumpkins how we did things in the big city. Of course, if I'd stopped to think about it for even half a second, I would have realized I didn't have the slightest idea how things were done in the big city, or anywhere else for that matter. Except for family events, this was the first party I'd ever been asked to attend.

Bob was already dressed when I came out of the bathroom. He was wearing black Levis, very tight around the ankles, a white dress shirt with a skinny tab collar buttoned up tight and black Beatle boots with pointy toes, stacked heels and zippers up the slides.

At home, that look had died out almost as fast as it had come in. Here in Fairweather, I supposed style trends came and went a little more slowly. I started to crack wise about Bob's get-up, but then I remembered he was my ride and kept my opinion to myself.

In the car, on the way over to Rhonda's house, Bob said, "Have you stopped even for a minute to ask yourself just *why* you got invited to this shindig?"

I knew he was setting some kind of trap for me, but I wasn't sure just where it was. "Well, I know it's not because I've taken Fairweather by storm. I mean, I'm not stupid."

"Okay."

"I guess I figured she felt a little sorry for me, not really knowing anybody and
all, and decided to do me a favor. Maybe she was just being nice."

"Sure, and maybe she invited me because I sing like Elvis Presley," Bob said. We pulled up at a red light. Bob lit a cigarette and inhaled deeply.

"Look, I've lived in this town all my life. I've known Rhonda Rutherford since the beginning of grade school and I can tell you, one thing she ain't is a nice person. If she invited you to this party, she's got a reason. Now I don't have a clue what it is, but if you're smart, when we get there you'll keep your eyes open and your mouth shut. And maybe this'll work out okay and you'll make a few friends and you won't get into any trouble you can't get out of."

I knew he was just trying to be helpful, but something about what he was saying, or maybe the way he was saying it, rubbed me the wrong way.

I said, "Bob, I appreciate you trying to help me out. And I know you know these people better than I do, so please don't take this the wrong way, but I really think I can get through this without you holding my hand."

"Suit yourself, but don't come crying to me if this all comes back to bite you in the butt."

Rhonda Rutherford lived in a part of town Bob called Snob Hill. One trip through the neighborhood and I understood why.

The houses were big and handsome and set back from the road on lots that were shaded with trees that could have been a hundred years old.

Almost every driveway held at least one expensive car and it was easy to tell which ones belonged to the kids. I saw GTOs and Mustangs and Corvettes, plus a few European sports cars parked next to the grownup Buicks and Chryslers. Compared with where Grandmother and Granddad lived, or for that matter, my own neighborhood at home, this was a whole different world. On this street Grandmother's ancient green Buick was as out of place as a patch of crab grass on a putting green.

Although we were on time to the minute, Bob and I were not the first to arrive, so we had to cruise about halfway down the block to find a place to park. When we rang the bell Rhonda's mother answered the door.

"Why, hello, Bob," she said, smiling. "We haven't seen you for a while. Come right on in." She turned to me. "And you must be Gary." She gave me an even bigger smile.

"Yes ma'am," I said. "Thank you for inviting me."

"Oh my, and you're so polite. Well, you are certainly welcome. Bob, I know you've been here before, so you can just take yourself and Gary out back by the pool. That's where all the kids are."

We headed down a long hallway that led to a set of double doors at the opposite end of the house. The doors opened onto a patio where there was a swimming pool and about twenty kids who were seated at several big tables talking and laughing. A few of the girls had taken off their shoes and were sitting around the edge of the pool, dangling their feet in the water.

Nobody was actually in the pool swimming, and I breathed a sigh of relief, as nobody had said anything about bringing swimming suits. I turned to say something to Bob, but he had spotted Bonnie talking with a group of girls on the far side of the pool and immediately took off in her direction.

I looked around for a familiar face. I saw a few people I remembered meeting, but nobody I knew well enough to start a conversation with.

Left on my own and with no one else to talk to I wandered over to an empty table and sat down. Earlier I had been excited about getting asked to come, but now that I was there, I began to think it hadn't been such a good idea after all.

I sat for a few minutes, listening to the Beach Boys music coming from the record player just outside the door into the house. Several more kids showed up, including a few I remembered meeting at the drive-in, but nobody came over to say hello. I was not surprised that neither Lee nor Rabbit nor Darby had been invited, though I wished they had. At least I would have had somebody to hang with. That's when I realized that Rhonda's party wasn't like an eighth-grade dance, with anxious girls on one side of the gym and dorky boys on the other. This party was for couples, and the only dateless dork at this party was me.

I was thinking about some way I could make an early exit when Rhonda and another girl walked over and sat down across the table from me. I couldn't think of the other girl's name, but I remembered meeting her at the A&W the night I arrived in Fairweather. Rhonda was carrying two glasses of lemonade, which she placed on the table next to me.

"Hi, Gary, I'm glad you could come. I'm sorry I didn't come over earlier to welcome you. It seemed like every time I started heading your way somebody else was coming through the door wanting to say hello."

"That's okay," said. "I was just making myself comfortable. And thanks again for having me. This is a great place you have here."

Rhonda said, "Gary, I'm sure you remember my friend Paulette. She heard about how you almost got killed at the car race the other night and I said, well, I heard that too. It sounds like it must have been a really terrifying experience. Why don't we go over together and ask him what happened?"

"It wasn't as bad as it sounds. A couple of cars crashed into one another and a wheel came off one of them. It flew into the stands, but it didn't actually come that close to me. I was sitting with another guy and we were already heading down to get a hot dog when the wreck happened. I guess if we hadn't moved right then it might have turned out a lot worse, but as it was nobody got hurt."

Rhonda gave me a puzzled look. "I didn't hear there was anybody else with you. Was it one of Bob's friends?"

I said, "No, it was somebody named Gideon. I've seen him around a couple of times, but I don't see him here tonight. Maybe you know him?"

"I don't," said Rhonda. "I don't believe I've ever met anybody by that name."

"Me neither, but I'm sure if he was anybody special one of us would know him," Paulette said.

"Well, I don't know if it makes him special to anybody else, but he's pretty special to me. If he hadn't gotten me to get up and move when he did I would have been wiped out for sure."

The girls looked like they didn't quite know what to say, and I realized I might have been a little too sharp with the tone of what I had said.

"Don't worry about it. Nobody else seems to know him either. Maybe he's just a figment of my imagination," I said.

There was an awkward silence and then Rhonda said, "Well, I see some more friends coming in, so I'm going to have to excuse myself for a little bit. Now I know you two will have a million things to talk about, so I'll just get back to my hostess chores and leave you to get better acquainted."

I would have settled for just one thing to talk about. I tried to think of something clever to say, or at least something that wouldn't sound stupid.

"Hi again, Paulette, I'm Gary Seiler," I said, failing on both counts.

"Paulette Conner," she said, holding out her hand for me to shake. "It's nice to *formally* meet you this time. We all heard Bob's nephew was coming down to stay for a while, and since Bonnie and I are best friends, which means Bob and I are friends, I wanted to be sure to say hello." She picked up one of the glasses of lemonade and took a small sip. I noticed her lipstick left a little smudge on the rim of the glass.

"I must say, you look much too grown up to be Bob's nephew. I thought Bonnie was talking about somebody a lot younger."

"Everybody says that. Bob is my dad's younger brother. They're more than twenty years apart," I said.

"That must have been quite a surprise for your grandparents." Paulette brushed a strand of hair away from her face and smiled. She was pretty, with reddish-blond hair, a splash of freckles across her cheeks and eyes a shade of blue that looked almost lavender.

I smiled back at her and drank some of my own lemonade. It tasted funny, like it needed more sugar. Then I remembered something and took a quick look around the back yard.

"When I met you at the drive-in, weren't you with somebody?"

She made a face. "That was Albert. He's not here tonight. We broke up."

"Sorry to hear it."

"Don't be," she said. "He's a jerk. It just took me longer than it should have to realize it."

I couldn't think of anything to say to that, so instead I asked, "What is it about Bob and Bonnie? Why does he have to sneak around to see her?"

"Ask Bonnie's father," Paulette said. "It's his problem."

"I don't think that would be a good idea," I said. "I get the impression from Bob that he doesn't think much of my family."

"It's not the whole family, it's just Bob. See, around school, Bob's got what you might call a reputation. He's had a lot of girlfriends, and until Bonnie came along, none of them were with him for very long. But he's never done anything bad, if you get what I'm saying. I mean, we all go to the same school and hang out with the same people and if somebody is doing something he shouldn't, word gets around pretty quick. I think Bonnie's dad is judging Bob by his reputation more than anything he's actually done, and that doesn't seem very fair, don't you think?"

"I don't know, I guess not. I've never had to worry about anything like that." I took another drink of lemonade. I didn't like the way it tasted, but I was stuck again trying to think of something else to say.

"It was awfully nice of Rhonda to invite me," is what I came up with. "I mean, this is a great party and she sure has a lot of friends."

"Yes, she's really sweet, and so pretty, too."

I don't know what came over me in that instant, but before I could pull back, I blurted out, "You're prettier. You have beautiful eyes."

Oh no! Did I just say that? Dear God, what was I thinking?

Paulette's eyes grew wide, the way Darby's had at the golf course, and I knew I had screwed up again. I held my breath. I waited for her to laugh at me. I waited for her to pour her lemonade over my head. I waited for lightning to strike me dead. But that's not what happened. Instead… she smiled. Not a pitying smile, but a real, warm, genuine smile.

"Tell me about yourself, Gary Seiler. Are you just like your Uncle Bob? Do you have a whole flock of girlfriends back home?"

"More like one I wish I had. There's this girl Wendy I like a lot, but so far not much has happened. I think about her a lot, but I haven't thought of a good way to tell her how I feel."

"Well, maybe I can give you something else to think about for a while," she said, and to my astonishment, leaned over and kissed me.

Not a peck on the cheek like you get when you visit your aunt on her birthday, but a kiss full on the lips that you remember for the rest of your life as the first time a girl ever kissed you.

"Come on, let's dance."

We got up and walked over to where other couples were dancing to "My Girl," by the Temptations. It was a good choice, too, because I am not a very good dancer except for slow songs. Also, I was feeling a little unsteady on my feet.

After the Temptations, another slow song called "Moon River" began playing, so Paulette and I danced another dance. About halfway through the song, she put her arms around my neck and laid her head on my shoulder. I slipped my arms around her waist and pulled her close.

This was definitely not the way I had learned to dance in my gym class at school, but when I looked around, all the other couples were moving together in exactly the same way. As the music continued, I started to get a funny feeling all over. Something was going on that I knew I shouldn't be involved with, but it was too late to back away now. I remembered Bob's question in the car on the way over and concluded that the reason Rhonda had invited me was so I could keep Paulette company while she was getting over breaking up with Albert. Nothing else made sense, and from the way things were going, it looked as if Bob had been worried about nothing.

About nine o'clock, Rhonda's mom and dad brought out trays of food, including hotdogs, hamburgers and pizza. When the adults made their appearance, I noticed that a lot of the kids put what they were drinking down in places where the cups and glasses could not easily be seen.

"So, what do you think of Fairweather so far?" Paulette asked between bites of pizza. "Being from the city, our little town must seem pretty boring."

"It seems like a great place to me," I said, a little louder than necessary. "Half my neighborhood could fit right here in Rhonda's back yard."

"Hmm. I thought city people were all rich."

"We're not. My dad's a rate clerk for the Frisco Railroad. About all that gets us are free rides on the train."

"What does a rate clerk do?" she asked.

"Like this. Say you have a factory and you want to ship what you make to a customer. You call the railroad and a rate clerk figures out how much it's going to cost. It's based on weight and distance."

"That doesn't sound very exciting," she said.

"My dad doesn't think so, either. That's why he wants me to go to college. But if he doesn't get better there won't be any way to pay for it. Then I'll probably end up working for the railroad just like him."

"It doesn't sound like that's what you want to do."

"I don't know what I want to do." I started to say that right now my main worries were Dad getting better, starting my freshman year in high school in the fall and Wendy. But then I remembered I was supposed to be almost sixteen, not fourteen and change, and so I said nothing.

"I know something you might want to do," Paulette said. She took my hand and led me to the back part of the yard. It was darker there, and I could see other couples sitting close together on the lawn.

Still holding my hand, Paulette tucked her legs beneath her and laid down on the grass. She kicked off her shoes and pulled me down next to her. "You didn't do too bad before, but let me show you the right way to kiss a girl."

It is impossible to describe the next few minutes. Kissing Paulette was not like anything I had ever experienced before, but to say it was exciting would be like saying that jumping out of an airplane without a parachute might be frightening. At one point I was startled by a burst of bright light. Someone had used a flash to take our picture and I thought *well, that's not cool*, and then they took a second picture. I looked up just for a second to see what was going on, and that's when I did the absolutely unthinkable.

I threw up.

Things happened fast after that. Paulette jumped up and began shouting, which made people come running to see what had happened. Somebody brought a pitcher of water and splashed it in my face. Then Bob found me, and he and another guy got me up on my feet and walked me around to the front of Rhonda's house. A few minutes later I was in the back seat of the Buick. The windows were down, and we were moving fast. The air blowing on my face felt good, but the motion of the car made me feel like I might throw up again at any minute.

My first thought was that I was on my way to a hospital. But then I looked around and realized where we were going. Five minutes later I was sitting on my grandparents' front porch, and the Buick's taillights were disappearing down the road.

The front door was locked and the house was completely dark. In the car, Bob had said something about where a key was hidden, but then he didn't tell me where it was, so I had no way of getting in without waking Grandmother and Granddad, something I definitely did not want to do. And since there wasn't anything else I could do, I stretched out across the glider swing and went to sleep.

CHAPTER FIFTEEN:

One Hot Car

The next thing I knew it was morning and I was still on the glider swing, cramped and shivering from being outside all night. Bob was standing over me. The expression on his face was a mix of amusement and admiration.

"Well, boy, I got to hand it to you. That was quite a night you had there. I expect half the people in town are talking about you right about now."

I groaned. "What time is it?"

"About six-thirty," Bob said. "What are you doing still out here, anyway? Why didn't you go inside and go to bed?"

"No key. I don't live here, remember?"

"There's a key hanging up above the door," Bob said, pointing. "It's been up there since your dad was a little boy. I told you where to look for it when I dropped you off. Guess you weren't paying attention."

"I guess not." I sat up. My head was pounding, and my stomach was turning cartwheels. "What happened? Did I get food poisoning?"

Bob laughed. "Food poisoning, that's a hoot. You got snot-flying drunk."

"What? No way. The only thing I had to drink was lemonade," But then I remembered the odd flavor I had noticed when I had my first glass. It seemed to go away after that. At the time I assumed somebody had just made a fresh pitcher, but in fact what happened was that I had simply gotten used to the taste of the spiked mix.

"Okay, what was in it?"

"Grain alcohol," Bob said. "Some folks call it Everclear. It don't taste like much, but it packs quite a wallop if you don't go easy, which you surely did not."

"Tell me about it," I said, holding my head. "Did I do anything really stupid, like throw up on somebody?"

"Yes and no. You threw up all right, but you managed not to get it on anybody else. I wouldn't worry too much about it, though. You weren't the only one that overdid it. You were just the first."

"The first what, or is it better if I don't know?" We both looked up and there was Grandmother standing in the front doorway. "And what are you two doing out here at this time of the morning?"

Bob said, "Well, we woke up early and were just fixing to go out and get some breakfast over at the pancake house. We're sorry, we didn't want to wake you and Dad."

Grandmother gave us a steely look. "Bob, for somebody that lying comes to as easy as it does you, it's a wonder you still ain't any good at it. I was awake most of the night waitin' for you two to get home. And since neither of your beds has been slept in, I'd say that's something you're just now getting around to."

Bob tried to look repentant, but even I could tell it was an act. Grandmother could read him like a billboard; he couldn't tell a convincing lie if he was talking to the neighbor's dog.

I said, "The party ran late, Grandmother, and you're right, we're just now getting home. It was my fault. Bob was ready to go, but I met this girl and we were having a good time and I wanted to stay a little longer, so we went out after the party."

"What girl?" Grandmother asked.

"Her name is Paulette. She was very nice to me."

Bob coughed and looked in the other direction. Grandmother eyed me suspiciously. "Was it her that upchucked on you, or was it the other way around?" She pointed to my pants legs.

"I did that, Grandmother. Rhonda's mom served a lot of spicy food at the party and I got sick in the car on the way home. I'll clean this up myself."

I wasn't sure whether Grandmother believed any of that or not, but she gave me the benefit of the doubt and let is pass.

"Your mom called last night, Gary. We talked for quite a spell and I mentioned the conversation you and I had. We agreed it was time to let go of what happened all them years ago. Also, she had some news about your dad."

"Is he better?" I asked.

Grandmother shook her great gray head. "I'm sorry to tell you there ain't been much change. About the only good thing that happened was that the other night after your mom went home from the hospital, the nurses said they heard him talking, but it didn't make much sense. They tried to get him to say something else, but it was no use. He just spoke up the one time and that was it."

"What did he say?" I asked.

"Well, nobody wrote it down, so they might not have it word for word, but your mother said they told her it sounded like 'Something is going to happen. We have to get away now.' It didn't mean anything to her. Does it mean anything to you?"

"Not a thing," I said, and a cold chill ran down my back.

*   *   *   *

Later in the day after Bob and I got cleaned up and caught a couple hours sleep, Lee came over and he and Bob finally bolted the 348 into the Chevy and cranked it up. At first the big V8 didn't run very well, but after they uncrossed two misconnected spark plug wires and adjusted the carburetor, it settled down into a reasonably smooth idle.

Of course, it was hard to tell by listening since there were just the exhaust headers coming off the engine with no pipes and no mufflers. The racket was enough to raise the dead, and it was more than enough to bring Granddad running from inside the house.

"Boy!" he shouted over what sounded like marbles rattling around inside a coffee can, "Don't even think about taking that bucket of bolts out on the road until you get it quieted down. And shut it off in the meantime or we'll have the police on the front porch before I finish my cup of coffee."

I had to hand it to Granddad. For a small man who never seemed to have much to say, he didn't have any trouble making his wishes known. Bob seemed hesitant to turn off the ignition, as if he were afraid he might not get it started again. But the look in his eyes reflected real pride that he had gotten the thing running in the first place. Granddad did his part not to spoil the moment.

"You boys done good," he said. Then he took out his wallet and handed Bob two twenties and a ten. "Go get some mufflers for that thing. When you get 'em hooked up, I expect you'll want to show me what she can do." Then he went back inside the house.

Bob and I climbed into Lee's Ford and the three of us headed downtown to a Western Auto store where Bob picked out a pair of glass-pack mufflers, six feet of straight exhaust pipe and enough clamps, gaskets and hangers to hook up the whole shebang to the headers and attach it to the underside of the car. Two hours later, after a lot of crawling around in the dirt and some colorful language from Lee, the born-again Chevy was ready for its maiden voyage.

Bob got behind the wheel and fired up the engine again. This time it started easily and settled into a considerably quieter idle. Lee claimed shotgun and I stretched out across the back seat as Bob pulled out of the side yard and steered the gray '51 toward the four-lane.

The Chevy didn't have license plates, so we had to take it easy on our way out of town in order to avoid attracting any attention from the Fairweather police. Along the way we made one stop at a filling station to fill the tank with premium gas. At thirty-two cents a gallon it wasn't a cheap fill-up, but Lee said since it was a high compression engine the 348 wouldn't run right on regular.

Bob said, "This is the station where Lewis Tate used to work. You remember, that's the colored fella we were talking about the other day?'

"I remember. Did he ever turn up?"

"Still missing," said Lee. "But I heard that now the sheriff is looking into where he might have gone off to. His family has filed a missing persons report. They think something might have happened to him."

"What do you think?" I asked.

"Personally, what I believe is that he probably did what everybody else like him does. When they don't have a job and they got bills they can't pay, they just pack up and leave town."

"But they don't take their wife and kids with them?"

"You watch and see. A dime will get you a dollar that in a few days they'll be gone, too."

"Gone where; to another town or the bottom of some river like those civil rights guys down in Mississippi?"

Lee turned in his seat to face me. "You know, it's a good thing you're Bob's nephew and not mine or we would have had to tangle by now, so you could learn some manners. It's like I told you the other day, you need to spend more than a few weeks here before you start passing judgment on how things are done in Fairweather."

I started to say something else, but I caught Bob looking at me in the rearview mirror. He didn't have to say anything for me to understand what he meant, which was, *let it go.* So I sat back in my seat and didn't say another word.

A few miles later we were outside the town limits. Bob came to a stretch of highway that ran straight as a string for about two miles. He brought the Chevy gradually to a stop, downshifting the four-speed transmission through third and then second gear. Lee took off his watch and studied it intently for a few moments.

"Ready," he said, and Bob began revving up the 348. He held the RPMs steady at 2,000 as Lee counted down.

"Three, two, one, now HIT IT!"

Bob popped the clutch and hammered the gas at the same moment. The results were spectacular, as the rear wheels broke loose and the car fishtailed a foot to one side and then the other as the tires clawed for traction. Then they took hold and we were off like a rifle shot, leaving in our wake a thick cloud of tire smoke and the smell of burning rubber mixed with unburned 104 octane gas.

From the back seat I kept an eye on the instrument panel over Bob's shoulder as we made our run. When the engine reached 5,500 RPMs, Bob slammed the transmission into second and then yelled out "Sixty."

Lee replied, "Seven seconds."

Bob upshifted to third and shouted, "There's a hundred."

This time Lee said, "About sixteen seconds."

We had gotten up to about 120 when a car turned onto the highway about a quarter mile ahead of us. Bob backed off the gas and stepped hard on the brake. When he did, it was like riding a tilt-a-whirl as the Chevy instantly pulled to the right, swerving off the highway and onto the gravel shoulder.

For a second, I thought we were going to smash right through the guard rail, but Bob yanked the steering wheel to the left and the car lurched back onto the pavement. Once we were back on the hard surface he was able to hold the Chevy on a straight course and bring it to a gradual stop.

"Son of a…." Lee breathed. "That was close! That needs to be fixed right away or the first time you go racing on the River Road you're going to need a tow truck to pull what's left of you out of the water."

As it turned out, Bob never did fix his brakes and Lee's prediction came terrifyingly close to coming true.

For the time being, however, it had taken coming within inches of a fatal car crash, but Lee and I managed to find something that we both saw exactly the same way.

CHAPTER SIXTEEN:
No Secrets

When Bob and I got home from the test drive there was a letter from Wendy waiting for me. Grandmother had placed it on top of the dresser in the guest bedroom.

My heart jumped the way it used to when I first saw the packages under the tree on Christmas morning, and I wanted to open it right away. But then I got nervous. What if she didn't like the letter I had sent her? What if she was just being polite writing to me in the first place? What if I had made a complete fool of myself in saying I wanted to get to know her better?

I sat on the edge of the bed for a long time, holding the unopened envelope in my hand, preparing myself for what I was sure was going to be a total letdown. Finally, I got my courage up and tore it open. Like her first letter, it was written on blue stationery and had the scent of flowers.

Dear Gary,

I was very happy to receive the letter you sent a short time ago. I'm sorry your summer isn't turning out the way you probably wanted, and I know it must be hard trying to fit in with a lot of people you don't know. I hope you are able to come home soon, because that will mean your dad is getting better. I know you must be terribly worried about him.

The reason that I didn't answer sooner is that I needed time to think about what you said, and what I wanted to say back to you. I know that some girls are very open about their feelings, but I have never been that way. I guess that's because I am afraid that if I say what I really feel to somebody I don't know very well, I could end up getting hurt and I don't want to have that happen to me. At the same time, I know that you took a chance writing to me as you did. So, after thinking about this for a long time I have decided that I will trust you in return.

In your letter you said that you liked me a lot, and Gary, I was thrilled to hear that. I must have read it twenty times the day I got it, and I still read it several times a day. Like you, I have never known anyone I wanted for a boyfriend, but I think that you are that person.

Since you were honest with me, I will be honest with you and tell you one more thing. I have never kissed anybody before, at least not in a serious way (my family doesn't count), and I would like for the first person who kisses me to be you. I can't tell you how scared I am to write this because I know you could use it to hurt me, so Gary, if you are not the person I should be saying this to, please tear up this letter and forget you ever read it. If you are the right person, please come home soon.

I can't wait to hear back from you.

Love,

Wendy

       *   *   *   *

That night Bob had a date with Bonnie. He offered to take me into town, so I could hang around with some of his friends, but I said no thanks. I would spend the evening with Grandmother and Granddad.

We watched television for a while, but since Fairweather only got one station from Tulsa and one from Springfield, Missouri, there wasn't much on. It didn't take long before I got bored and went outside to sit on the porch.

Grandmother didn't like the smell of tobacco in the house, so Granddad had to go outside every evening and smoke his pipe before he went to bed. He liked to sit in an old rocking chair that I never saw anybody but him ever use. I sat on the glider swing and kept him company.

It was a warm night, and it felt good just sitting in the dark smelling the aroma of Granddad's pipe tobacco. All around the yard fireflies winked at one another and the air was alive with the sounds of crickets, birds, cicadas and other nocturnal creatures. For a long time neither of us spoke.

Finally, I said, "Granddad, can I ask you a question?"

"Anything you want as long as it don't make me late for supper." That was his little joke, and he never got tired of it.

"No, but it might have something to do with money."

"Go ahead."

"Well, I was just wondering. When we went to church last time, I noticed we were sitting in a pew that had our name on it. And then after, at the restaurant, it seemed like there were a lot of people who came up to you and Grandmother and they…" I stopped, not sure how to put the question.

"You're wondering why all those fancy-looking folks are acting nice toward your Grandmother and me?"

"Well, I guess so, yeah. It's like when Bob and I went to that party at Rhonda's house last night, I noticed the same thing. I mean, the kids there all seemed like rich kids, and Lee and Rabbit weren't there, so I was wondering what's so special about Bob and me that we got invited."

Granddad chuckled. "What's special about you is you're with us. What's special about us is we've got more money than they do. Or at least your grandmother does. Her people used to be in the manufacturing business back east and when they passed, your grandmother inherited most of what they left behind. It's worth close to three million dollars today."

Three million dollars? Our family has three million dollars?

"But if you have all that money, how come Dad never said anything? And why don't you live, you know, in a better place?"

"Well, I expect because your dad didn't see any reason for you to know. And as far as why we live here, this is where we've always lived. We've raised our boys in this house, and your grandmother and I have an understanding, which is that since we don't need the money for anything else we're saving it for your dad and your uncles for them to share after we're gone. Someday, I expect some of that will get handed over to you and your cousins. Split that many ways it might not make you rich, but it'll be a nice nest egg for you when you're older."

My head was spinning as I struggled to connect three million dollars to my own reality.

"The reason all them other folks go out of their way to talk to us is because the one place we do give a little money is the church you visited, and they're all hoping we'll give a little more. Plus, there's always this good cause and that needy organization, and they figure if they're nice to us maybe we might help them out a little."

Granddad paused to re-light his pipe which had gone out while he was talking. "Don't misunderstand, Gary. I'm just a poor boy from Oklahoma, but your Grandmother is from quality. People put up with me because I'm hitched to her."

"So that's why Bob gets invited to their houses," I said.

"That's it, like that deal you two went to last night." He stopped rocking and leaned forward in his chair, lowering his voice so Grandmother wouldn't hear. "Speaking of which, I understand that party got a little out of hand."

It wasn't a question, so I didn't bother pretending that I didn't know what he was talking about.

"Maybe a little," I admitted. "It wasn't too bad."

"It wasn't too good, the way I heard it. Listen, I'm not your pa, and it's not for me to be telling you what to do. So, I'll just say that if I was you I'd try to take it a little easy while you're down here. We'd like to send you home in at least as good a condition as you were in when you got here."

"I'll try, Granddad," I said, and I really meant it.

He was quiet for a moment. "Bob's girlfriend there, was she?"

Now I had to be careful. I had no idea how much Grandmother and Granddad knew about Bob's plans for the future, and I didn't want to be the one to mess things up for him. But Granddad read my mind.

"It's okay," he said. "I don't mean to put you on the spot. Your grandmother and I already know about Bob signing up for the Marines, and we also heard he was fixing to ask his girl to get married."

I didn't know what to say. "He told you?"

"No, Bob didn't, but the sergeant down at the recruiting station did. Right after Bob left they gave me a call. Wanted to know if it was all right, since Bob ain't but seventeen."

I was stunned. "You said it was okay?"

"I said they could have him as soon as he was eighteen, if that's what he still wanted to do. Naturally, your grandmother wasn't too happy, but Bob's about to be a grown man and I expect he can live his own life however way he wants."

"So, then it's okay with you if he gets married, too?"

Granddad laughed out loud this time. "It's the same thing as with the Marines. Soon as he's eighteen he can do whatever he wants. Of course, we brought him up right, just like your folks did with you. We trust him to do the right thing."

Granddad got up from his rocker, came over and rubbed his hand across the top of my head. "I'm going to call it a night and maybe you'd best, too. Tomorrow's going to be an early day."

CHAPTER SEVENTEEN:
A Discovery

The next morning Granddad got his first and—as it turned out—his last ride in Bob's hotrod Chevy. Before Bob left for his date with Bonnie, Granddad announced that the three of us were going fishing the next morning and Bob was going to do the driving. Of course, since the trip was to take place on Sunday, that also meant that Grandmother would be going to church without any of us.

Bob didn't have an excuse ready, so I was pretty sure he hadn't seen this coming. But I also got the feeling that if the choice came down to fishing or church, the fish would come up a winner every time. And so, half an hour before sunrise Bob,

Granddad and I were heading down Highway 69 toward Granddad's favorite fishing hole.

We stopped at a gas station where Granddad bought three dozen nightcrawlers, a bag of ice, some bread and sliced ham, a small jar of mustard and several bottles of orange pop. Bob bought five more gallons of gas for the Chevy. Once back in the car Granddad made himself comfortable in the back seat. I rode up front with Bob.

When we were well outside of town, Granddad said to Bob, "Okay, let's see what she'll do."

Bob let the car coast down to about twenty miles an hour, downshifted into second gear and nailed the accelerator. Once again, the Chevy did what Bob had built it to do and in practically no time we were running a hundred miles an hour. Above the noise of the engine and the wind rushing past I heard Granddad let out a whoop of pure excitement. After all those years riding around at a snail's pace in the Buick, the tire-melting acceleration of Bob's '51 must have been a real treat.

Granddad said, "Okay, you can back her down now. And now that we all know how fast she'll go, just you make sure you don't go letting the sheriff know, too. Any tickets you get, you're on your own." And then he said, "This is quite a machine. You boys did a hell of a job." I could tell, and so could Bob, who was beaming with pride, that Granddad was impressed.

We got off the main highway near a town called Big Cabin and then drove down a gravel road to a location along the Verdigris River that Granddad called his "honey hole."

After Bob parked the car, we got the tackle and the cooler out of the trunk and spread out about fifty feet apart along the shore. Granddad said we'd have better luck if we didn't all fish in the same place. He said this was a good spot for catfish and another fish he called buffalo, but that there were lots of underwater snags, so he warned me to be careful and not let my line drift with the current.

Granddad showed me how to attach a sinker about a foot above the hook. Then I baited the hook with a nightcrawler and tossed the line out into the river. We were going to be fishing using a method he called "tight line." The trick, he said, was to always be sure that I could feel tension in the line, and if it started to move downstream, to reel in a couple of turns to keep the current from carrying it under a log.

"There's a lot of deadfall that goes into the river every time there's a big rain. The fish love it because it gives them cover, but them limbs will eat up a lot of tackle if you're not careful."

It wasn't long before I found out about that. I didn't have my line in the water more than five minutes when I felt what I thought was a bite. I got all excited, thinking I was going to have the first fish of the day. I grabbed the rod and set the hook, hard. The slack came out of the line and then SNAP! The line broke and the sinker, minus the hook, came flying out of the water like a bullet.

"Granddad, I got torn off. Do we have any more hooks?"

"Got you a log, I expect," he said without looking up from his own line. "Check in my tackle box. Take whatever you need."

I walked up the bank and opened Granddad's tackle box. It was a big one that opened in the middle, with three trays on each side. He had every kind of tackle you could think of: plugs, spoons, spinner baits, bobbers; it was like a portable bait shop. At the very bottom of the box was a leather bag closed on the top with a drawstring. I opened the bag and looked inside.

There was a small revolver.

I took it out and looked at it. The metal was blue steel and the grips were black plastic. On the barrel was stamped ".32 CAL S&W CTGE." I had been around handguns before, so I knew the lettering meant that the gun was a .32 caliber and used a Smith and Wesson cartridge. I also knew that since it was a revolver, it didn't have a safety and I could see that this gun was loaded.

I slipped the revolver back into the leather bag, closed it and replaced it in Granddad's tackle box. I found a hook the size I was looking for and walked back down to the bank where I had left my rod and reel. I tied the hook on the end of the line. Then I walked over to where Granddad was fishing to get another nightcrawler.

I said, "Granddad, why do you have a gun in your tackle box?"

"Thought you were looking for a hook," he said.

"I was. But you had so much stuff I just wanted to see what else was in there."

"It's okay, no harm done," he said. "As to why, it's in there for a couple of reasons. One is, there're some big snapping turtles in this river, and if you get one on your line there isn't but one way to kill it."

"Why kill it? Why not just cut the line?"

"If they're the right size, they're good eating, so you want to keep them. But you don't want to handle them any more than you have to when they're alive, because they can bite your

finger off like it was a peppermint stick."

"What's the other reason?"

"Same as why there's also a snake bite kit in

that box. I believe that no matter where I go or what

I'm doing, I want to make sure nothing bad happens

to the people I care about. Today that means you

and Bob. Other times it might be your grandmother

or somebody else. But no matter who's with me,

I'm going to do my best to look after them. I

learned that in the army. You look out for the

people who are close to you and you trust them to

look out for you. I tried to teach that to my boys,

and today's as good a day as any for you to learn it,

too."

I thought about that.

"Then why didn't Dad look out for us?" I

said. "Why didn't he take care of himself instead of

getting drunk and probably killing himself by

running into a telephone pole?"

I didn't wait for Granddad to answer my

question. Instead, I walked back down the bank to

where I had left my fishing rod. I rebaited the new hook and cast the line out into the murky brown water, a little closer to shore than last time. Then I sat down to wait for a bite.

*   *   *   *

We had been fishing for about three hours and had several nice catfish on the stringer, though we had yet to hook any of the fish that Granddad called buffalo. By late morning the sun had gotten hot and I had already gone through two bottles of orange soda plus sucked on a dozen or so chunks of ice from the cooler. I had to pee.

"You can walk on up that trail a ways," Bob said, pointing to a narrow path through the woods. "You'll have all the privacy you want."

I set my rod and reel down and trudged up the path Bob had pointed out. I had gone maybe fifty yards, taking care to watch out for poison ivy, which grew all over the place in the woods. As I walked, I heard a sound like an animal running through the brush. I thought I might have startled a

deer and waded into the thick undergrowth to see if
I could spot it.

As I got closer to where the sound had come
from I caught a smell, which grew stronger the
farther I went. The brush was very thick, and it took
a minute to locate where it was coming from. A
hundred or so feet off the trail I came to a small
clearing. What I found there was something out of a
nightmare.

It was a man, lying face down on the
ground. He wore no shirt and no shoes. His hands
were bound behind his back and something had
been wrapped tightly around his throat. His arms,
neck and ankles were horribly swollen. I had never
seen a dead body before, but it was obvious that this
one had been here for several days.

Up close, the smell was overpowering. I got
lightheaded and I thought for a second that I might
pass out. Then panic gripped me and I ran blindly
back in the direction of the path.

"Granddad, come quick!" I shouted. "Oh,
my God! Granddad, Bob, help!"

"Where are you?"

"Up the path, hurry, please hurry!" I shouted.

Bob got there first with Granddad puffing a short ways behind him. Granddad had his revolver in his hand.

"What's the matter?" Bob said. "You act like you seen a bear."

"This way," I said.

"Oh, Lord," Granddad said when we reached the clearing. "Oh, this can't be."

Bob said something a lot worse.

"I was walking up the trail when I heard an animal. Then I smelled something and came over here to see what it was."

"Well, you found out, all right," Bob said. "Wonder who he is?"

Granddad put his pistol into his pants pocket. "Well, I expect we'll have to turn him over and take a look. Then you boys are going to have to go for the sheriff. I don't see any other way to do it."

Granddad nodded to Bob. Bob hooked two fingers in the dead man's belt loop and carefully rolled him up on his side. Granddad stared for a moment. Then he stepped back and sighed. Bob let go of the man's belt loop and let him roll back onto his stomach. I could tell from their reaction that Bob and Granddad knew who the man was, and although I had never seen him before, I was pretty sure I was looking at the body of Lewis Tate.

There wasn't much more we could do after that. Bob and I drove back toward town until we found a gas station with a telephone booth, then called the sheriff's office. A few minutes later, a deputy drove up and we led him back to where Granddad was waiting. The deputy took our names and address and radioed for assistance and an ambulance to come and pick up the body. We went back down the path to where the car was parked and each of us gave statements to the deputy. Then we gathered up our fishing gear and drove back to Fairweather.

Not long after we got back and had told our story to Grandmother the telephone started ringing. Word had gotten out about the day's events and Bob's friends all wanted to hear the story. I thought we might hear from somebody at the sheriff's office wanting additional information, but that didn't happen. Granddad said he expected before long we would get a call from the newspapers in Tulsa and Oklahoma City.

After supper Bob was in a hurry to head into town to meet up with his friends. He asked me if I wanted to come along, but the image of Lewis Tate lying face down in the woods was still vivid in my mind, and I had no wish to relive the experience by telling the story over and over again.

So, I told Bob I was tired, and that I wanted to be by myself for a while. I think he was relieved to hear it, because my staying behind meant he would have the center of attention all to himself. As far as I was concerned, he could have it. At that moment, I wanted nothing more than to get out of Fairweather and go back home where I belonged.

CHAPTER EIGHTEEN:

Fight Night

The next morning at breakfast Bob was loaded with gossip from his trip into town. It seemed that everybody he talked to had his own idea about what might have happened to Lewis Tate.

Most of the theories ran along one of two lines.

The minority view was that he had been the target of a holdup gone wrong. It was true that his wallet and identification had been missing at the time we discovered his body. But I didn't believe for one second that he was a robbery victim, and I didn't think Grandmother or Granddad believed it, either.

The more widely held idea was that Mr. Tate's complaints about not being able to get his girls into a white school had finally gotten under somebody's skin to the point where, as some said, he "needed to be taught a lesson." However, nobody seemed to have a very good idea about who might have actually done the killing.

Bob hurried through his eggs and got up to put his plate in the sink.

"I need to talk to you for a second," he said to me, jerking his head in the direction of the front porch. "It's important."

I asked Grandmother to excuse me, then followed Bob out the door. Outside, clouds were gathering in the southeast, and I could hear thunder rumbling in the distance. The wind was beginning to pick up, and the smell of rain was in the air.

"What's up?" I asked.

"You know that girl you met at Rhonda's party the other night? Remember, the one that was being, well, sorta friendly with you for a time?"

"Paulette? Yeah, of course I remember, why?"

"Well, do you also remember a guy you met the first night you were in town? A real big fella, he was?"

"I remember."

"Well, in case you didn't get it the first time, his name is Albert and you know, Paulette and Albert, they're kind of a couple."

"You mean they were a couple. She told me they broke up."

Bob nodded. "That's right, they did. But now they're back together. And those pictures somebody was taking the night of the party, they were Polaroids. Those are the ones that come out of the camera and develop themselves."

"I know what they are," I said. "Let me guess. Somebody showed them to Albert and now he's pissed off at her."

"Not quite." Bob stared at a spot on the ground as if a snake were coiled there. "He's pissed off, but not at her. He's pissed off at you and now it looks like you're gonna have to fight him."

"What? No way, what does he want to fight me for?"

"Well, truth is, he wants to beat the hell out of you. He thinks you acted, um, improperly with his girl."

"That's crap. In the first place, I just went along with what she wanted to do. In the second place, she gave me spiked lemonade. And in the third place, she wasn't his girl at the time."

"Maybe so, but that's what you might call a technicality, because she sure is now," Bob said. "Do you remember in the car on the way over to Rhonda's house I asked you why you thought you got invited to that party?"

I did, and I also remembered that at the time I pretty much ignored the question because I thought I was smart enough to handle myself.

Obviously, I had been wrong. I felt the ground start to give way beneath me.

"It was to give Paulette a way to get back with Albert, wasn't it? That's why the pictures. I'll bet Paulette and Rhonda cooked this up, and they used me because I don't live here and wouldn't have enough sense to figure out what was going on."

"I'd say you hit the nail in the center of its head," Bob said, "except I don't think they expected Albert would want to come looking for you. They just thought it would be a good way to make him jealous."

"Well this is just great. When is this fight supposed to take place?"

"He says tonight, in the picnic area over at the park, right after the pool closes. He says if you're not there, then he'll come looking for you."

This was all too much, and I was having trouble getting my thoughts organized. I said, "How come you got appointed to tell me all this?"

"I imagine because you live here with me. Plus, I'm supposed to act as your second."

"What do you mean, my second? What is this, a duel?"

"It's nothing like that. Just a regular fight," Bob said. "I'm just supposed to make sure the fight goes off fair and square."

"Okay, then as my second, you can just go tell Albert and anybody else that's interested that I'm not doing this. As far as I'm concerned, he can just go to hell, and this whole town can go right along with him."

"Well, you might be able to say that, but I can't," he said slowly. "See, I have to live here and as far as most people are concerned, I'm responsible for you. So, if you don't show up, even if you got on the train and went back home right now, today, I would still be responsible. It'd be hard for me to hold my head up after that."

"So, this is about you? Are you worried that if I don't fight this jerk you might have to?"

Thunder rolled again, and I saw a streak of lightning in the southeast sky.

"No, I wouldn't have to fight him. But a lot of people would think poorly of me because I didn't keep you under control any better than I did."

"Oh," I said hotly. "In two months, you're going to ship off to Parris Island to learn how to fight the Communists, but you're not brave enough to ignore what your precious friends might say about *me*? Some Marine you're going to be."

Bob hesitated for a moment, and when he spoke his voice was cool. "Truth of the matter is, you might have some of this coming. Since the day you got here you haven't had one good thing to say about Fairweather or my friends or anything else. And when I tried to give you some advice when we were on the way to that party, you more or less told me where I could stick it.

"Well, that's all water under the bridge, but now you're going to have to pay the price for that crappy attitude of yours, and from the looks of things, tonight's the night."

Before I could say anything else, Lee pulled up in his Ford to take Bob to work.

"Listen," he said, his tone softening, "I wouldn't worry about this too much. It's mostly all for show. You just have to be there and let him shove you around a little bit. Tell him you're sorry, it won't happen again and that'll be the end of it. He'll look like a big man to his girl and people will respect you for not backing down. The whole thing will be over in a couple of minutes."

He tried to put his hand on my shoulder, in a gesture of sympathy, but I pushed it aside.

"Get away from me," I said. "Go kill a Communist."

The rain started right after Bob and Lee left, so there wasn't any work to do in the yard. Grandmother announced that after she dropped Granddad off at work that she was going to stay in town to do some shopping and attend a luncheon at her ladies' club, so I would be on my own for most of the day. At eight forty-five, she and Granddad huddled under a big black umbrella, splashed their way out to the Buick, and headed off toward town. That left me with nothing to do but try to think of a way I could get out of taking a pounding for kissing a girl that I didn't care anything about.

Maybe Bob was right. Maybe I did have it coming. If I hadn't been so cocksure of myself, I might have taken Bob's advice and kept my head low at Rhonda's party. Or, when I noticed that the lemonade I was drinking didn't taste quite right, I could have switched to something else that hadn't been spiked. Or maybe I could have just stayed home and avoided the whole mess instead of getting involved in some high school drama intended to patch up a shaky romance using me as the glue.

To take my mind off the situation, I tried reading the newspaper. There wasn't much there that was encouraging. Things were not going well in Vietnam, and President Johnson was talking about sending more troops. I also found a story about how the body of a man identified as that of Lewis Tate had been found alongside the Verdigris River in neighboring Craig County. The story said that the body had been discovered by fishermen but didn't include any of our names. The article went on to say that the apparent cause of death was strangulation but left out most of the other details. The story concluded by saying that the sheriff's department hadn't determined a motive, and that they had no suspects at this time.

After I finished the newspaper, I turned on the television and flipped back and forth between the two available channels without finding anything interesting. Finally, I did the only thing left that I could think of, and that was to telephone Darby.

"Do you see now why I don't have any use for boys?" she asked after listening to my story. "Although I can't imagine any girl ever wanting to get into a fight over me, either. What are you going to do?"

"What can I do?" I said. "Hide in the house, sneak out of town, or fight the guy."

"Hmm. Not very good choices, are they?"

"No, and it gets worse." I stared out the window as sheets of rain swept across the yard.

"Bob says if I don't stand up to this guy he won't be able to hold his head up in town."

"Well, now, that's Bob's problem," Darby said. "I don't see where you need to prove anything on his account, but maybe it would do you good to prove something to yourself."

I thought about that and decided she might be right. "You got any suggestions?"

"Well, I remember this one thing that Lee said to me when he got into a fight after a football game. It's risky, but it might work. If it doesn't, you're going to get beat up, but that'll happen anyway." When she told me what it was, I had to admit that she was right, it didn't sound promising. But it was all I had if I didn't want to hide in Grandmother's house for the rest of the time I would be in Fairweather.

Hard rain continued right through the afternoon. Grandmother got home from her meeting about 2:30 and went into her bedroom for her afternoon nap. An hour and a half later she was bustling around in the kitchen getting supper

started. Then she went out again to pick up
Granddad from work. By the time she and
Granddad got home, the rain had stopped, and the
sun was breaking through the clouds. More rain was
in the forecast for the next day, and the day after
that, but according to the radio it probably wouldn't
start until some time late the following morning.
That meant there wasn't going to be any rainout as
far as the fight was concerned.

The conversation during supper was mostly
about Lewis Tate.

Granddad said that the men down at the
Railway Express office thought that whatever had
gotten him killed, he had probably brought it on
himself. Best to leave things alone, they had said,
and let folks work out their own problems in their
own time. There was no need to be complaining to
the newspapers or trying to bring in demonstrators
from out of town.

I said, "Do you believe that, Granddad?"

He put his fork down and folded his hands
in front of him before he spoke. "No, I don't. Not in

this case. I think there's a time that comes when a person has got to stand up for what's right and do whatever it takes to get it done. Lewis Tate did that, and I'm sorry it cost him his life. But I also think there are enough good people in this county to see that the right thing gets done now. I think before the year is out, Lewis will get justice and so will his little girls."

"What happens if he doesn't?" I asked.

"Then there will be trouble. There was a time when a white man could get away with doing anything he wanted to a colored man and nothing would be done about it. But those days are over now, and if the law doesn't take its proper course, then I think some folks might decide to take it upon themselves. And that would not be a good thing for anybody."

When supper was finished I helped Grandmother clear the table. Then I went outside and sat down on the front steps to wait for nightfall. I felt like a condemned criminal waiting out the last hours before his execution. I was scared, I was angry, and the more I thought about it, the less sure I was whether I blamed Bob or my father for the whole situation.

If my father hadn't gotten drunk and wrecked his car, I wouldn't even be here. And as far as Bob was concerned, maybe I should have listened to him before the party, but as I saw it, I was the new kid in town. There was no way that I could have known any of the details about who was going steady with whom, and it was Bob's responsibility to steer me clear of all that. And if he couldn't, then at least he should have been able to figure out some way for me to avoid having to fight my way out of a jam he never should have let me get into in the first place.

I looked at my watch. It was nearly seven-thirty; an hour and a half to go.

After a while, Bob came out and sat down next to me. I moved over as far as I could to increase the space between us.

"You know, you could be worrying for nothing. Albert might not even show up."

"He will," I said. "He's in love."

We stayed there for a while longer watching the shadows creep across the lawn. Normally I would have enjoyed the evening coming on. The air smelled fresh from the rain earlier in the day, and the setting sun threw vivid streaks of orange, red and purple across the western sky. I tried desperately to think of some way to get out of what was coming. I could pretend to be sick, which wouldn't have been far from the truth, or I could "accidentally" fall down the porch steps and hurt myself so that I wouldn't be able to fight. In the end, though, I knew there was nothing I could do except show up and face whatever was waiting for me.

"Guess we better get going," Bob said at last.

"I guess so," I said. And then I remembered something that might give me a way out after all. I told Bob I'd be right along, but there was something I needed to do first.

When I went back into the house Grandmother and Granddad were in the front room watching television.

"Bob and I are going into town," I told them. "I just need to get something out of my room."

Grandmother must have heard something in my voice. "Are you feeling all right? You sound like you might be catching something."

"I'm fine," I said, and walked down the hall toward the back of the house.

Instead of going into my room, however, I ducked through the kitchen. As quietly as I could I opened the door to the cellar and went down the stairs. After a minute, I found Granddad's tackle box and the leather pouch that held his revolver. My hands shook as I broke it open to see if it was still loaded. Then I stuck it in my front pants pocket and pulled my shirt out, so it wouldn't show.

In the car on the way to the park I thought about what might happen next. I knew I wasn't going to shoot anybody. I supposed that if things got real bad and Albert seriously wanted to pound on me, I could pull Granddad's gun and try to scare him with it. Of course, I wouldn't do that unless Darby's idea didn't work, but the fact was, I really didn't have much confidence that it would.

When we got to the park there was a crowd of kids already gathered around the picnic area near the swimming pool. I recognized Rhonda and Paulette, who was wearing a bright yellow dress, as well as other kids I had met at the party or at Skelley's and the A&W. I also recognized the guy with his arm around Paulette.

Somehow, he looked even bigger than I had remembered.

Well, maybe this will be a one-punch fight. Maybe he'll hit me so hard that when I wake up I'll be back in St. Louis in the intensive care unit with Dad.

Bob went over to where Albert was standing with Paulette. He said something to Albert that he must not have liked because he pushed Bob roughly to the side. Then he turned to me.

"You start," he said, and began walking in my direction. My knees felt weak, but I stood my ground and let him come.

"This is your deal," I said. "Come and get me."

I kept my hands in my pockets, my right wrapped tightly around the revolver.

"What's the matter, you afraid?" he sneered at me.

"You're older than me, you've got me by fifty pounds, so yeah, I am, if that makes you feel good. But like I said, this is your dance, so go ahead and start the music."

I could hear the kids around us start to murmur. Somebody shouted, "You guys gonna do anything or not? I have to be home by midnight."

Albert looked around, not sure of himself, as if he was no longer confident his friends were with him and knowing he would have to make the first move.

He looked around again and then seemed to make up his mind.

He stepped quickly across the distance between us and hit me hard across the face with his open hand. For an instant I felt my eyes go out of focus and then a ringing noise started in my ears. That's when I got really scared.

"You ready to fight now, city boy?" he taunted. "Or do you need a little more motivation?" He moved in on me again. The sound of his shoes in the loose gravel covered the mechanical noise the revolver made as I cocked the hammer. Lights flashed inside my head as he slapped me a second time. This time I tasted blood, and whatever fear I had been feeling was swept away by a wave of anger.

The voices of the crowd faded away as did their faces and everything else around us. The only thing I saw was Albert and the only thing I heard was the blood pounding in my ears.

Overconfident, he advanced a third time. As he moved in, I pulled my right hand free of my pocket and hit him as hard as I could smack on the nose. It was a solid punch, and it caught him by surprise. The sensation in my arm was like grabbing hold of a live electrical wire. I felt the impact all the way up the length of my arm and into my shoulder, and I knew that in about five seconds either the fight was going to be over or I was going to be on my way to the hospital.

Albert put both hands over his nose, staggered backward a couple of steps, lost his balance and fell on his butt in the gravel. He groaned loudly and when he pulled his hands away, they were covered in blood.

"Damn, I think you broke my nose!" he howled, and quickly covered his face again with his hands. I reached back into my pocket and let the hammer back down on Granddad's revolver.

From behind me I heard a girl scream, "Albert!" followed by, "Don't hurt him any more!" and then I saw a yellow dress rush past me as Paulette ran to Albert and cradled his head in her lap.

She glared up at me furiously. "Look what you did to him!" she spat. "I hope you're satisfied."

I wiped a trickle of blood from the corner of my mouth. "I'm a real bastard," I said, and walked back toward the car.

Later, at the A&W I got a surprise. While I sat with Bob and Lee and Rabbit holding a cup of ice against the side of my face, Albert and Paulette pulled into the parking lot. Albert got out of his Mustang and walked over to where we were sitting.

Here it comes for real, I thought.

But Bob, Lee and Rabbit all closed in around me like bodyguards. If there was going to be any more trouble, I would not be fighting alone. Instead of cocking his fist, however, Albert stood at a respectful distance and held out his hand. His nose looked swollen and both his eyes had blackened.

"Paulette told me what happened at the party. She said she was just trying to make me jealous. She said she only wanted for us to get back together again. Well, we are, and now I'm sorry for the trouble it caused you. It wasn't your fault."

I accepted Albert's hand. "No harm done. Paulette's got herself a good man. You two look after one another."

Albert said, "Thanks. You take care, too." Then he turned and walked back to his car and the two of them headed off into the warm Oklahoma night.

Bob looked at me in amazement. "You are one lucky fella is all I can say. I thought for sure when you mashed his nose I'd be taking whatever was left of you home in a washtub."

"Actually, Lee deserves the credit. Darby told me something you told her after a football game and I took your advice."

"What was that?" Rabbit asked.

"Lee said that most bullies aren't used to the sight of their own blood, and that sometimes that's enough to stop a fight before it gets going. I was betting that Albert might be one of those people. He's so big that I figured hardly anybody ever actually fights with him. It was the only chance I had so I took it."

"I did tell her that," Lee said. "I'm surprised she remembered."

"I'm glad she did," I said.

Later, in the car on the way home, Bob was still talking about the fight, and how lucky I was that Albert hadn't beaten me half to death.

"The one thing you haven't said is, after you hit him, what was your plan if he'd have come up swinging?"

"That's a good question," I said. I took Granddad's revolver out of my pocket and placed it in my lap where Bob could see it. His eyes grew suddenly wide.

"You weren't really going to shoot him, were you?"

"No, I'd have fought him the best I could and then if there was anything left of me, maybe I would have shot you."

CHAPTER NINETEEN:
Cops

Bob and I didn't have much else to say to each other the rest of the way home that night, and things weren't any friendlier between us the next day.

I guess it shook him up when I took Granddad's gun out of my pocket and let him see it. Of course, I never would have shot anybody, and had made sure of it by unloading it before we left the house that night. My thinking had been that if things had started to go badly, I could have taken it out and pointed it at Albert, and maybe that would have been enough to get him to back off. I was scared of getting hurt, but not scared enough to shoot him, or Bob for that matter.

The next morning it was raining hard, and Bob was hoping he might get the day off from working at the park. But his boss called early, saying he needed him and his crew to check the storm drains around town to make sure they didn't get covered over with debris and start backing water up into people's yards and basements.

At breakfast, Grandmother noticed that the side of my face was swollen and that there was a bruise around my right eye.

Before I could make up a convincing story, Bob said, "Gary got into a little bit of a fight last night."

Granddad put down his coffee cup and looked at Bob. "What kind of a fight?"

I held my breath, expecting the worst.

Bob shrugged like it was nothing. "Aw, you know how things happen. Gary and this other fella, I don't know his name, they were talking about something and this other boy called Gary a name, which I will not repeat, and Gary said, 'That's it,

I'm done talking to you,' and this other boy hit him upside the head and said, 'You don't walk away from me, plowboy,' and the next thing you know, Gary's got him down on the parking lot and gave him what for. You'd have been proud."

Later, while we were cleaning up the breakfast dishes, I said to Bob, "Plowboy?"

"Your granddad hates that term. I could have told him you shot that fella and I doubt he would have minded." He turned and looked at me without smiling. "'Course, I don't know how you would have shot anybody with a gun that didn't have any bullets." When I raised my eyebrows at that, Bob said, "After we got back last night I went down and checked the tackle box. Guess you're not as stupid as I thought."

I hoped Bob would be heading into town after work that night. We still weren't on the best of terms, but I wanted to go along, thinking that I might see Gideon and possibly clear up one more mystery. However, looking after the storm drains kept Bob at work until well into the evening, and by the time he got home he was too tired to do anything except take a shower, eat and collapse into bed.

The sun came out on Wednesday morning and I was able to get Grandmother to drive me to the golf course after she dropped Granddad off at work. Darby had something else to do, so I played nine holes by myself. Unfortunately, there were big puddles of water all over the course and it was hard to play a normal round.

Still, I was hitting the ball well and was beginning to think I might actually have a chance to make the golf team in the fall.

When I finished, I called Grandmother and she came and picked me up. I treated her to lunch at the clubhouse, and then on the way home we stopped at a drug store where I picked up a couple of cards to send to Mom and Wendy.

When we got back to Grandmother's house there was a sheriff's department car parked out front. Grandmother drove up to the gate and I got out and opened it so that she could pull the Buick into the side yard. When I went back to close the gate, a man got out of the patrol car. He was dressed in a tan uniform trimmed with brown stripes down the pant legs and brown epaulets on the shoulders. He wore a Stetson hat with gold insignia on the front. He was about my father's age, but taller. He waited for Grandmother to get out of her car, then walked over and introduced himself.

"My name is Deputy Crowley," he said, touching his right hand to the brim of his hat. "I'm with the Craig County Sheriff's Department. Are you Mrs. Seiler?"

"I am," said Grandmother. "How can I help you?"

"Actually, I wanted to talk to your grandson." He turned to me. "Are you Gary?"

"Yes, sir," I said. At first, I thought this might have something to do with the fight on Monday night. Maybe Albert had changed his mind about being a good sport and had gone to the police about his broken nose. But then I remembered that Fairweather was in Ottawa County, and in an instant, I knew what this officer wanted to talk about. Big Cabin, where Bob, Granddad and I had gone fishing on Sunday morning, was in Craig County.

He said, "Would it be all right if we went inside?"

Grandmother invited the deputy to sit on the big sofa in the living room. I sat in an armchair to the deputy's right. Grandmother pulled a straight-backed chair from the dining room table and sat down facing both of us.

"Deputy, can I make you some coffee?" Grandmother asked.

"No, thank you. This will only take a minute."

The deputy took off his hat and placed it on the couch next to where he was sitting. Then he took a file folder out of a case he had been carrying.

"Gary, I wanted to ask you a couple of questions about what happened when you were fishing the other day. But before I do, I wonder if you could just tell me again how you happened to come across Mr. Tate there in the woods."

I went back over the story, explaining how we had been fishing and that I had to go to the bathroom, so I walked up the trail to find a private spot. I heard what sounded like animals rustling around in the bushes and then I smelled something, and when I went to see what it was, I found Mr. Tate.

"Okay," the deputy said. "That checks out with what I have here. Now, since that day, have you thought of anything you might want to add to that?"

"I don't understand," I said.

"Well, for instance, had you ever met Mr. Tate before the day you found him in the woods?"

"No sir. I heard people talking about him, but I'd never actually seen him."

"Who did you hear talking?"

"Well, there was my Uncle Bob and some of his friends. They all thought Mr. Tate had left town to try to find another job since he had gotten fired here."

"That was all?"

"Yes, sir, it was."

"Tell me something else, then. When you went into the woods looking for an animal you thought you heard, did you see anybody else, you know, maybe looking for the same thing?"

"No."

"Or maybe you saw something, like a wallet or something like that?"

"If I had, it would have still been there when the other deputy came."

"Unless it got moved, or somebody picked it up and forgot to turn it in," he said, looking me in the eye.

Grandmother spoke up. "The boy has told you what he knows. Now I have a question for you, and that is, what are you doing about finding out what happened to that poor man besides asking my grandson a bunch of questions he's already answered?"

The deputy ran his hand through his short hair. "We have set up a task force with the State Police and the Ottawa County Sheriff's Department, and to tell the truth, I wouldn't be surprised if the FBI decided to get involved. They might want to treat it as a civil rights case, which would give them federal jurisdiction. As far as we're concerned for right now, it's a homicide case. My job is to re-check the leads we've already got."

I said, "Does that include going back over where the body was found?"

"Of course," the deputy said. "Why?"

"Well, for one thing, I don't remember seeing any signs of a struggle. I mean, if somebody was trying to kill me, I'd be fighting to my last breath, but the ground around him wasn't torn up at all. That makes me think he wasn't killed where we found him. If that's so, then somebody had to carry him there, and I don't see how one person could do that. I remember that path is very steep, and it's hard enough to climb up when you aren't carrying anything, let alone something as heavy as a dead body."

"So, you think more than one person was involved?"

I looked at Grandmother, then back at the deputy. "Don't you?"

He sighed. "You're probably right, and the task force is looking at it that way, too. But I don't think we're going to solve this on our own. I think it's more likely that some time down the road somebody will get to bragging about how he got away with murder. Then word will get around and we'll finally be able to make an arrest. Until that happens, I think it's going to remain an open investigation."

Deputy Crowley thanked Grandmother and me for our time and assured us we would be kept informed about any progress with the investigation. Then he got back into his car and drove away. It was the last time the police would ever speak to anyone in our family about the murder of Lewis Tate.

Later that afternoon I sat down and wrote the two cards I had picked up earlier in the day. I wrote Mom's first:

Dear Mom,

Grandmother told me you called the other day to say that Dad doesn't seem to be getting any better. She also said that Dad spoke a few words the other night. This is going to sound creepy, but there is a guy I met down here named Gideon who said almost the same words to me Dad said in the hospital, and he said them on the same night!

Mom, I really want to come home. Grandmother and Granddad have been great, but however things are going to turn out for Dad, I want to be home and not here when it happens. I think I have a right to be there.

Gary

I thought for a long time about what I wanted to say to Wendy. What I finally came up with was this:

Dear Wendy,

I have read your letter every day since I first got it, and I promise I will never use it to hurt you or embarrass you. I just wrote to Mom and asked her if I could please come home soon. Of course, I want to be home because I am worried about Dad, but also because I want us to be able to spend the rest of the summer together.

If I don't hear from Mom in the next few days I will call her and try to talk her into changing her mind. In the meantime, I am thinking about you and looking forward to the day that I will be able to see you. Keep your fingers crossed that it will be soon.

Love,

Gary

That night, it started to rain again, hard.

CHAPTER TWENTY:
Revelations

The rain kept up for most of the next day, and Bob and Lee had to work pumping rainwater out of the sand traps on the golf course. The newspaper, the radio, and even the two television stations were warning of flash floods in the low areas.

There was a small creek about half a mile from my grandparents' house that was barely a trickle most of the time, but when I walked over to look at it on Thursday afternoon, the water was up near the top of the banks and moving fast. I knew there wasn't much danger of it reaching any of the nearby houses, but the sight of the muddy torrent churning past was a little bit frightening. I shuddered to think what the chances would be of surviving the experience for anyone or anything unlucky enough to fall into that water. And then I remembered something.

*   *   *   *

It was the same summer Dad and Mom had taken Aunt Edna and me to the Lake of the Ozarks. The first day we were there Dad drove us all down to the dock where the resort kept its rental boats. Dad wanted to rent a rowboat and take us around the lake for a while, but first I wanted to try a canoe by myself.

The wind was blowing, and Mom wasn't happy with the idea, but Dad said, "Why not? If he wants to try, he should go for it."

So, Mom paid a dollar for half an hour and off I went.

I paddled out until I was about a hundred yards from the dock, and then Mom started to get nervous about how far out I was and called for me to turn around and come back. I tried to turn the canoe the way Dad had showed me, but when I did, the wind caught it. It did a quick spin and just as quickly I was in the water. I tried to swim to shore, but I was too far out. I panicked and began thrashing around, swallowing water as I did so.

As I started to go under I felt strong hands take hold of me and pull me to the surface. Then Dad began splashing his way back to the dock, carrying me under his arm. The amazing thing about that was that Dad couldn't swim very well, but even so, he managed to reach me and bring me back to shore.

He risked his own life to save mine.

    *   *   *   *

Bob was late getting home from work again, but instead of heading off to bed right after supper, he got cleaned up to go into town.

As he was heading out the door I said, "I'm coming with you."

He looked at me coolly. "I don't recollect inviting you."

I said, "Fine, just drop me off at the A&W. After that, I can get around on my own and you can go do whatever you want."

We rode most of the way into town in silence. Bob smoked a cigarette and fiddled with the radio he and Lee had installed in the Chevy a couple of days earlier. They must have left an electrical connection loose somewhere, as the sound kept cutting in and out whenever we hit a bump in the pavement. Finally, he gave up and switched it off.

I felt a sudden urge to ask a question that had been unanswered since the night I hit town. "So, when are you getting married?"

"What?"

"When are you and Bonnie getting married? Before or after you ship out?"

Bob flipped his cigarette out the window "Don't know for sure."

"How can you not know?" I said, "You did ask her, right? I mean, we talked about this the first night I got here."

"I asked her," he said.

"And what did she say?"

"She said she wasn't about to marry anybody who hadn't finished high school. She said without a diploma there wasn't going to be any way I would be able to support a family."

"She has a point," I said.

"Also, she said I'd have to quit smoking."

"There's that, too," I said.

"And finally, she said she wasn't going to waste a good wedding on somebody who was fixing to ship off with the Marines and get himself killed in Vietnam. So, I told her it didn't make no matter whether I enlisted or finished high school, because either way I'd be going in. Only difference is whether I sign up now or wait and get called up."

He was right about that. I wasn't completely sure how it all worked, but the only way Bob was going to avoid getting drafted was if he either couldn't pass a physical exam, or if he went to college. Neither of those seemed likely to happen.

Bob dropped me off at the A&W before heading off down Kansas Avenue toward Skelley's, his usual spot for meeting up with Bonnie.

"You sure you'll be okay by yourself?" he asked, gunning the Chevy's big V-8 impatiently.

"I'll be just fine," I told him. "Don't worry about it." The truth was, I preferred not to have him hanging around. I had a feeling my days in Fairweather were winding down and I wanted to see Gideon once more before I had to go. To do that, I felt I needed to be by myself, or at least as much as I could be in a parking lot full of kids and cars.

I walked over to the picnic bench where I had been sitting the first time I met Gideon and waited. I scanned the parking lot and the faces of the kids, hoping to pick him out of the pack. Finally, someone noticed me and began walking my way.

"Hi, Albert," I said.

"Howdy. Are you here by yourself?"

"I was until just now," I said. "What about you?"

"The same, I'm afraid." He sat down on the bench next to me. "Paulette and I broke up again. This time I'm thinking it's for good."

"I hope this hasn't got anything to do with me," I said. "I'm all through fighting."

He shook his head. "It's a long story, but it pretty much comes down to she's not ready to settle down with me. I was just one in a long line of guys."

"I'm sorry to hear it, Albert, I really am, but my dad says in the end things always work out for the best."

"I guess. Say, if you aren't doing anything special, a bunch of us are going up to Kansas later. There's this place right over the state line where they don't check IDs. We can have a few beers and maybe get us a race later on."

I said, "Thanks anyway, Albert. I appreciate the invitation, but I remember what happened the last time I tangled with alcohol. Since the party, my grandparents have been keeping a pretty close eye on me. If they get the idea I've been drinking again they might just lock me in my room for the rest of the time I'm here."

"Well, if you're sure," he said.

"Yeah, I'm sure," I said, "at least for tonight. But thanks anyway." We shook hands again and he walked back to his Mustang.

I sat on the picnic table for another hour, but Gideon never showed up. I spoke to a few other kids who either wanted to talk about the fight with Albert or me finding a body in the woods. By eleven o'clock, most everybody had cleared out, and I started thinking about how I was going to get home. It was close to a five-mile walk and it looked like it might start to rain again. However, just about the time I figured I was going to have to call Grandmother to come get me, I spotted Lee and he offered to give me a lift.

In the car, Lee said, "What's the matter, Bob run off on you?"

"No. He had something he needed to talk over with Bonnie, and I didn't want to be in the way."

"Well, he took her home an hour ago. Last I heard was he and some boy from Vinita had a race set up down on the River Road. Do you want to head out and see if they're still there? He's pretty proud of that Chevy."

"No, I don't think so. Bob and I aren't exactly seeing eye-to-eye just now. He might not appreciate me checking up on him."

Lee laughed, not in a friendly way. "You do seem to have that effect on people. As you've probably figured out by now, this here is a small town. You got to be careful how you act around people in a place like this. You get out of line and folks won't want to have nothing to do with you. Get too far out of line and you might end up out in the woods with a length of baling wire wound around your neck."

I thought at first that he was just making a bad joke. Then I remembered something that made my head start to spin.

I said, "Lee, who told you that it was wire that was used to murder Lewis Tate?"

There was a pause. "I don't recall. Saw it in the paper, I guess."

"I don't think so," I said. "I read everything I could find, and there wasn't anything about rope or wire or anything else."

"Well then, Bob must have told me."

"Yeah, maybe he did, that was probably it," I said, but I knew he was lying. At the time we found him, Lewis Tate's neck was so swollen there was no way to tell what had been wrapped around it.

We came to a stoplight. Lee sat quietly, drumming his fingers on the steering wheel, thinking. The next move was up to me.

"I wrote my mom a letter yesterday," I said. "I told her I was having a good time, but I thought maybe I needed to come home."

"I think you're right about that," Lee agreed. "And if it was up to me I'd say the sooner the better. You seem to have a way of gettin' under people's skin."

It was past my grandparents' bedtime when Lee dropped me off, so there was only a single yellow bulb illuminating the porch and the front steps. Otherwise the street in front of the house was completely dark. Before Lee drove away, I turned and leaned in the open window on the passenger side of his car.

"Lee, Bob didn't tell you Lewis Tate was strangled with wire because he didn't know. I didn't know myself until just now." I waited for him to say something. When he didn't, I said, "You don't have to answer me, but I do have to ask you. Do you know anything about who might have murdered Lewis Tate?"

Again, there was no answer. Finally, I said, "Look, I don't know what happened to Mr. Tate the night he died. Maybe you don't either; I hope not. But it seems to me if there's something you're not telling, you ought to do the right thing and come forward. Don't you think his family deserves that much?"

I stepped away from Lee's car and watched him drive off. Then I walked up the front steps, reached the key down from on top of the door frame and let myself in. I put the key back in its place and locked the door behind me. Not wanting to wake my grandparents, I crept down the hall as quietly as I could. Then I got undressed and climbed into bed.

It was a long time, however, before I was able to get to sleep.

CHAPTER TWENTY-ONE:
Water

I'm not sure what woke me up. I think it was the silence. My grandparents' house, as old as it was, was a symphony of small noises, even in the middle of the night. The roof creaked as it cooled after the sun went down. The windows rattled in the wind, the kitchen faucet dripped, and the big exhaust fan in the hallway ceiling rumbled and roared like an airplane taking off. Outside, the yard was filled with sounds made by birds and insects calling to one another in the darkness.

And then, suddenly, it was as if someone had flipped a switch and cut off every one of those sounds, filling the house with total silence. It was

the same thing that happened at the race track, right
before the accident that nearly killed me.

I opened my eyes and looked around my
room. Someone was standing at the foot of the bed.
I couldn't see his face, but his voice carried a tone
of urgency.

"Gary, I'm sorry to wake you, but we have
to go. Bob needs help right now."

"Gideon?" I sat straight up in bed and
rubbed my eyes. "What's going on? How did you
get in here?"

"The key over the door, remember?"

I was awake now, and frightened. "How do
you know about that?"

"It's been there for forty years. I'm afraid
Mom and Dad are creatures of habit."

"Who are Mom and Dad? Gideon, I don't
get it. What's this about?"

"You'll understand soon enough," he said.
"Come on, we have to go. And keep your voice
down. We don't want to wake anybody."

I got out of bed, pulled on my jeans and shirt

and stepped into my sneakers. Then, like I was walking on glass, I followed Gideon down the hall and out the front door. As we crossed the porch and went out into the yard I could see lightning streaking across the sky in the southeast. It was about to rain again, and from the way the wind was picking up, it wasn't going to be long coming.

Gideon handed me a set of car keys and pointed to the Buick. "You drive."

I took the keys but made no move toward the car. "I think we'd better wake Grandmother. I can't drive this thing. I don't even have a license."

"You can drive it. Now come on, get in. There isn't time to waste."

I got into the car, put the key into the switch and turned the ignition on. Then I pushed the accelerator to the floorboard to engage the starter. The noise from the wind whooshing through the trees drowned out the sound of the Buick cranking over. I slipped the gear selector into drive and eased forward toward the gate. Gideon undid the latch and swung it open. I pulled out onto the road and waited while he closed the gate behind me.

Instead of getting into the car, he ran around to the door on the driver's side and motioned for me to open the window.

"Aren't you coming?" I asked.

He shook his head. "You go on ahead. I'll be right behind you."

I looked around but didn't see another car. "Where am I going?"

There was a bright bolt of lightning, and the first drop of rain splashed heavily against the windshield. The full force of the storm was just seconds away now.

"You remember the first night you were here, when you went to watch the race?"

"The River Road, you mean? Is that where Bob is?"

Lightning danced again, and the rain began coming down in torrents. Although it didn't seem possible, in the momentary light I noticed that although Gideon was standing in the downpour, he didn't appear to be getting wet.

"Just take it slow," he said. "Start looking when you get to the finish line, and don't worry, I'll be there. Now go."

I slipped the Buick into DRIVE. The rain was coming down so hard that even with the windshield wipers running on high speed it was nearly impossible to see where I was going. The one good thing about that was that with poor visibility I was less likely to attract the attention of any police who might otherwise wonder what a kid was doing driving around Fairweather in an ancient Roadmaster at three in the morning.

I took the familiar route out of town until I came to the River Road turnoff where the new highway veered away from the original road. During the twenty minutes it took to get there, the rain had let up, so that even though I didn't know what I was looking for, now at least I had a chance of seeing it. I passed the finish line painted on the pavement that marked the end of the River Road race course and still hadn't seen anything.

I rounded the last curve, just ahead of the point where the old road rejoined the highway. Not far away I spotted a lone figure standing on the shoulder of the road, waving his arms over his head. As I pulled to a stop and rolled down the window he ran up to the side of the car. It was Gideon, right where he said he would be.

"Is it Bob?" I asked.

"He's down there!" he shouted, pointing to a spot just ahead where the white-painted wooden guard rails were broken off. Tire tracks were visible in the gravel before they disappeared down the embankment and into the darkness. I remembered from the first night I was here that river was about thirty feet below the roadway at this location. I also remembered the crappy brakes in Bob's car that he had never gotten around to fixing.

"What happened?" I asked.

"You can see for yourself. He must have lost control and crashed right through the guard rail there. Come on, you have to get him out."

"Gideon," I said, "you knew about this. Why didn't you do something before now? Why is this up to me?"

"Because I can't help Bob," he said. "I can only help you."

I thought about the prospect of trying to climb down the bank in the dark. "How do you know he hasn't already gone into the river?"

"I don't, but we have to try to save him if we can," Gideon said. "Look, maybe you should stay out of this. It might not be as bad as it looks. You take the car and head back to the highway. Find a phone and call the police. They might be able to get here in time."

"No, there's no time for that," I said, shutting off the engine. "If I can save Bob, then you can save me. We'll get him out together."

"I'm sorry," he said, "you'll have to do it alone. At least until he's safe."

"I understand," I said. And in that moment, everything became clear, and I knew what I had to do.

In the dark it was impossible to make out what we were heading into. Once beyond the broken guard rail the ground sloped abruptly downward toward the water. From all the rain we'd had in the past week, the river was well above its usual level, and with the storm that had just ended I knew it would be coming up even further. Gideon and I made our way down as quickly as we could. I was in the lead, but it was slow going as I had to pick my way through mud and undergrowth.

I judged I was about halfway down when my feet slid out from beneath me and began skidding toward the water. I tried to grab onto something to stop my fall, but all I could catch hold of were weeds that either pulled out of the ground or slipped through my muddy hands. At the last moment, my feet caught on something solid. I reached out with my left hand to steady myself and felt cold steel. It was the Chevy!

At that moment, the clouds momentarily parted and the moon, directly overhead, cast a colorless light over the scene. The Chevy had overturned as it crashed down the embankment and had come to rest on a ledge that was still about two feet above the surface of the river. It was lodged against a tree, which is what had prevented it from sliding all the way into the water. The passenger side was facing me, but the door was partly buried in the mud so that it was impossible to open. The driver's side was hanging out over the water. Steadying myself against the side of the car, I was able to get to my knees and look inside.

The car was a mess. There was dirt and weeds and broken glass scattered around, and a tree limb the thickness of my arm had come through the windshield and broken off as the Chevy had taken its wild ride down the riverbank. I could see Bob inside, lying on his back on the headliner. His right leg was bent above the knee at an odd angle, and I knew for sure it was broken. I reached inside and shook his shoulder.

"Bob?" I called, but he didn't answer. I put my hand over his chest. His heartbeat felt strong, but he was unconscious, either from pain or some other injury that I couldn't see. "Bob?" I called again.

Just then I felt the Chevy move. I knew what was happening. The water was rising, and it had started to undercut the bank where the car was lodged. It wouldn't be long before the bank gave way and the Chevy with Bob still in it would be swept away with the current.

From somewhere above me I heard Gideon call, "Gary?"

"I found him!" I shouted back. "He's passed out, though. I've got to get him out of here now!"

"All right, I'm coming down. Just hang on until I get there."

"There's no room. We'll just get in each other's way. Look, if you're really here to help me, go call the police. There's nothing you can do here."

Having nothing solid to hang on to, I unbuckled my belt and pulled it free. I groped around on the ground until I found a sapling that I hoped would be rooted deep enough not to rip out of the wet ground. I looped the free end back through the buckle then knotted it around the trunk of the sapling. I slipped the other end around my ankle and crawled partway inside the Chevy, praying that everything would just stay put for another minute.

The wind picked up again, the moon disappeared back into the clouds and there was a flash of lightning. In that instant I could see that the river was only inches from the open window on the passenger side. Once the current got inside it would spin the car around and suck it into the muddy water. There was not another second to spare.

By stretching as far as I could, I managed to get my hand around the waist of Bob's jeans. Then I tensed my body and began dragging both of us backward, out of the car. The movement was enough to strain Bob's broken leg and to rouse him back to consciousness. There was another flash of lightning, and more thunder.

Bob screamed in pain.

"Bob!" I shouted. "Bob, can you hear me?"

"I hear you, only you got to stop tugging on me. I think my leg's broke!"

"I know, Bob, it's busted and that's that. Now listen. In about two minutes this car and everything in it, including you and me, is going into the river, so we have to get you out now. You're just going to have to hang tough for another few seconds. This is going to hurt like hell but there isn't anything I can do about it until we get you out of there. Do you understand me?"

"Tell me what I need to do," he groaned.

"Okay. I want you to reach up and grab the edge of the roof right here. When I tell you, try to pull yourself out the window. I'll pull at the same time, and maybe we can get you out of there."

Thunder rolled heavily, and rain began falling again. Our time was just about up.

"Bob, do you understand what I said?"

In response he reached up and took hold of the door frame with his right hand. I tightened my grip on the waistband of his jeans. One pull was going to be all we would get. If this didn't work, it would be all over.

"Okay, here we go, NOW!"

Lightning flashed, thunder rolled, and Bob and I pulled, each of us yelling as loud as we could, him with pain and me with exertion. The effort was enough to drag his upper body and his hips through the window. At the same moment, the car began to tilt away from us. Almost noiselessly it slipped down the bank and into the river. As the car fell away, Bob came free, like toothpaste from a tube, leaving us both sprawled in the mud barely a foot above the rushing water.

Bob's pride and joy with its hot 348 engine rolled over once in the current and disappeared into the turbulent water of the Neosho River.

Careful not to lose my grip on him, I got to my knees. I reached my arms under his and clasped my hands across his chest. Then I slowly crawled backward on my knees and elbows until I felt the tension go out of the belt that was still looped around my ankle. I reached back with my left hand and took hold of the sapling where the belt was tied. I used that for leverage to pull us both a few feet farther back from the edge of the river.

"Bob, are you okay?"

"Ah-h-h-h, I'm okay, I guess, except for my leg. I reckon I'll live."

"Don't be too sure," I said. "We're still not out of this. What happened here, anyway?"

He groaned. "I was on my way home when I pulled up next to a fella at a red light. He gunned his engine and I gunned mine and next thing you know, we had a race set up. So, we came down here. I thought Lee was following me, but I guess he had something else to do. Well, we took off and he got out ahead of me and then I saw something on the road, a deer, I think, so I hit the brakes and just like the other day the car pulled right and next thing I knew I was upside down in the woods."

"The other car didn't stop?"

"I don't think he saw what happened, or if he did he didn't want any part of it. I bet right now he's back home congratulating himself on what a fast car he's got—hey, wait a minute! What are you doing here, anyway? And how'd you know where to come looking in the first place?"

Good question. "It was late and you weren't home. I had a hunch. I came looking," I said. "Would you rather I hadn't?"

He started shivering, and I was afraid he was going into shock.

I said, "Bob, I don't think I can drag you out of here by myself. This bank is just too steep. Here." I undid the looped end of the belt from my ankle and slipped it over his arm. "I want you to hang on to this until I can get back down here with some help, okay?"

He nodded, and I could see the pain in his face. "Okay, but hurry. I'm hurting pretty bad."

It took some doing on the muddy slope, but I was able to climb back up to the side of the road. With Gideon gone for help, my job would be to flag

down the police when they arrived. When I reached
the top, however, the Buick was still sitting on the
side of the road. Gideon was leaning against the
front fender on the passenger side.

"Why are you still here?" I had to shout over
the noise from the rain and the river rushing below.
"You were supposed to go for help."

"Already done," he told me. "Help's on the
way. Listen." He paused, and I could hear sirens
approaching in the distance. "They'll be here in just
a minute."

"Then I guess I'd better get on up to the
intersection to make sure they don't pass us by," I
said. "And I guess our business is finished."

"I expect it is," he said, and for a moment
we stood, not knowing what else to say.

"Am I going to see you again?"

"Not for a long, long while," he said. "Not
until it's time. But don't worry about a thing.
Everything is going to be just fine."

"I know that now," I said, "and thanks."
And there, with the rain pouring down, I shook his

hand one last time. Then I began walking toward
the highway to wait for the police.

CHAPTER TWENTY-TWO:
Forgiveness

The rest of the day flew past like scenery outside the window of a moving train. By the time I got back with the police, Gideon was gone, as I knew he would be. I learned later that a local resident who was checking the level of the river had seen the Buick parked next to the broken guard rail. Guessing correctly that there had been an accident, he hurried home and telephoned the police.

Luckily for Bob, the two officers who arrived on the scene were able to carry him back up from the river to the side of the road. They immediately sent for an ambulance, and within fifteen minutes he was on his way to a waiting emergency room. Luckily for me, with everything that was going on the police took my name but didn't ask for any identification. Otherwise I would have been on my way to a waiting juvenile detention facility as an unlicensed driver. Instead, they let me get back into the Buick and follow the ambulance to Ottawa County General Hospital.

While doctors looked Bob over, I ducked into a restroom to clean up. By the time I finished, Grandmother and Granddad were in the waiting room, having been brought by another police car. They did not look one bit happy.

Despite my protests that I was fine, Grandmother insisted that one of the doctors give me a quick once-over. In fact, I was a patchwork of cuts and scratches from battling my way first down to Bob's car and then back up to the road again. A nurse treated my wounds with iodine and band-aids, including one that required a couple of stitches. After the nurse pronounced me fit, Granddad sat with me in the waiting room while Grandmother went to look in on Bob.

While we were waiting for news of Bob's condition, I explained how the night's events had unfolded. Granddad listened without interrupting until I finished.

"So, you're saying this Gideon fella just showed up in your bedroom and told you Bob needed help?"

"That's right, Granddad."

"And while he was at it, he told you where to look?"

"He did, but the River Road is one of the places I would have tried anyway," I said. "Lee brought me home earlier, and he said Bob had run into somebody who was looking for a race. I just figured that was where they'd be likely to go."

Granddad was quiet for a moment. "So, this Gideon, do you have any idea where he is now?"

"Gone back to wherever he came from," I said.

"Do you figure to hear from him again?"

"He said not for a long time."

"Or find out who he really is?"

"Oh, Granddad, don't you know? Really, don't you know?"

"I guess maybe I do, Gary. But if I'm right, then I expect we're going to be getting a call from your mom before another day passes. Have you thought about that?"

I nodded. "I think—I think that maybe what this was all about was his way of making up for something he felt he should have done before. I think maybe he was trying to make things right."

"You think he wanted to put things right with you?"

"No, Granddad, with himself."

Granddad said, "Bob owes you his life, you know. He's going to feel like he needs some way to pay you back. And so far as that goes, so will your grandmother and so will I."

"Nobody needs to pay me back, Granddad. I just wanted to do the right thing, the way Gideon did. It's like you said. You look out for the people you love and count on them doing the same for you."

We sat silently after that, each of us lost in our own thoughts. Another hour passed before Grandmother reappeared with news about Bob. She looked exhausted from the strain of the night's events, but her voice was filled with relief.

"He's got a broken leg. The femur, it's called. That's the big bone up in his thigh. It'll heal in time, but he'll probably walk the rest of his life with a bit of a limp. He's also got a broken collarbone, a broken wrist and a punctured lung where a couple of his ribs went through it. He'll live, thank the Lord, but I expect he'll be laid up for quite a while.

"As for you," she said, turning to me, "what kind of shape are you in?"

"I'm okay, Grandmother. I wasn't in a wreck."

"No, but you could have been." She looked at me over the rims of her glasses. "I didn't know you knew how to drive."

"Dad taught me," I said.

"Well, he did a good job. You know, I can't help thinking that I ought to be mad at you for something, but I don't know what, and I'm too worn out to think about it. So, I'll just say I'm thankful. I'm thankful that you saved my boy and you did it without getting yourself killed." And to my surprise, she bent over, took my face in her big hands and kissed me gently on the forehead.

"Now let's go home. Bob's going to be out like a light for quite a while, so I reckon we might as well go back to the house and get some sleep ourselves. I have a feeling this is going to be a long day."

I said, "Grandmother, you know Bob's car went into the river. I'm pretty sure it's going to be a total loss."

"Don't worry about that," Granddad said. "Somebody will fish it out in a day or two and tow it back home. It'll give Bob something to do with his hands while he's on the mend. I might even go out and hold the wrenches for him."

When we walked out into the hospital parking lot, instead of asking me for the keys to the Buick, Grandmother said, "You drove it this far. You might as well drive it on back home."

And so, with Grandmother and Granddad both in the back seat holding hands like a couple of teenagers on a first date, I drove the old Buick back home and parked it carefully in the yard.

*   *   *   *

The call Granddad and I were praying we would not get came just before noon. Grandmother, who was in the kitchen preparing lunch, answered the phone.

I heard her say "Hello," then "Yes," then "Tell me," and then she made a stricken sound. When she handed me the telephone, tears were coursing down both of her cheeks.

On the other end of the line, Mom said, "Honey, I'm so sorry. Your dad died this morning."

I spent the rest of the day packing up my stuff for the trip home. Mom had booked me a reservation on the *Meteor*, the night train back to St. Louis. This time I would have my own bedroom in a Pullman car.

Ordinarily, I would have been excited to finally be going home, and to be traveling in a sleeper, but now that what we had all feared had actually happened, I would have gladly stayed the rest of my life in Fairweather if it had meant not making this trip.

At suppertime Uncle Ronald and Aunt Virginia came by my grandparents' house. Aunt Virginia had prepared a chicken dinner which we all shared around the dining room table. The chicken was delicious, but nobody seemed to have much of an appetite so most of it wound up being left overs.

Around ten o'clock Uncle Ronald offered to take me to the train station in Vinita, where I boarded the *Meteor* an hour later.

Before I left, I hugged Grandmother and Granddad, although it wasn't a difficult parting since I knew I would be seeing them the next day in St. Louis. The only thing I missed out on was

saying good-bye to Bob, as he was still sleeping off
the medication he had been given during the surgery
to repair the damage to his lungs.

When I got to my room, the porter had
already made down the bed, so there was nothing
for me to do but brush my teeth and climb under the
covers. I thought at first it might be hard to sleep, as
the room was tiny and the car made lots of strange
noises as it rocked and rolled over the steel rails
beneath us. But the events of the last few days
caught up with me quickly, and the next thing I
knew the porter was knocking on my bedroom door,
telling me we would be arriving at my stop in half
an hour.

Mom was waiting at the station in Webster
Groves as the train pulled in. She hugged me for a
long time and then, while my luggage was being
unloaded from the baggage car we sat on a bench
outside the depot. There were a million things I
wanted to tell her, but I could see there was
something she wanted to say, so I kept quiet and
waited for her to get to it.

After a while, she cleared her throat. "I spoke to one of the nurses yesterday, after I called Grandmother, so she doesn't know this. The nurse told me that Dad talked again, just before he died. She said she was making her rounds and had just walked into Dad's room to change his I.V. when he sat up in bed. The breathing tube was out of his mouth and he looked at her and said the strangest thing."

"I know. He said, 'Don't worry. Everything is going to be just fine.'"

"That's right." Mom looked at me strangely. "How did you guess that?"

"I heard him," I said. And then I told Mom about Gideon.

*   *   *   *

Dad's funeral was a big one. There were friends, and people from the railroad and relatives from both sides of the family. Grandmother and Granddad drove up from Fairweather with Uncle Ronald and Aunt Virginia. Uncle Warren and Aunt Judy came over from Kansas City and, of course, all the relatives from Mom's side. Bob was still in the hospital, so he wasn't able to be there, but Granddad said he had wished he could, and even sent a card expressing his condolences. I knew that must have been hard for him, because although I had lost my dad, Bob had lost his brother.

A lot of my friends were there as well, including Phil and Wendy, and even some of my teachers from school. I didn't really have a chance to talk to any of them during the visitation because I had to stay close to Mom, but it was great that so many people cared enough to come and pay their respects.

In the weeks following, we learned it wasn't the injury Dad suffered from the accident that killed him, nor was his drinking the cause of the accident. Instead, it was a cerebral hemorrhage—a stroke— that caused him to lose control of his car, and ultimately to lose his life.

As I had expected when Dad was first injured, Grandmother and Granddad stayed with us at our house, and sure enough, I wound up on the couch in the living room.

The first morning they were there Mom and Grandmother sat down for a long conversation across the kitchen table. There was a lot of discussion about hurtful things that happened a long time ago as well as promises about how they were going to be in the future. However, what caught my attention in a big way was that Grandmother promised Mom that when the time came, she and Granddad would make sure there would be money for me to go to college if that was what I wanted to do. Grandmother said that the money would be ours to share some day anyway, and that there was no reason for us not to have a little bit of it now, when it would do us the most good. It was a funny thing, but in a way, Dad's death had served to bring our family together in a way that would not have happened if he had recovered. I guess you could say it was his legacy.

The day after the funeral, after the relatives had all said their good-byes and headed for home, I got on my bike and rode three miles to Wendy's house. We went out into her back yard and sat on the lawn facing one another in the shade of a big silver maple tree.

Wendy held my hands in hers as I told her the story of my summer with Grandmother and Granddad, Bob and Lee and Rabbit, Paulette and Albert, Darby, and finally Gideon. And then at the end, when my story was finished, she put her arms around me and held me close.

And for the first time since the accident back in June, I cried for my father.

EPILOG

August 12, 1965

Dear Gary,

I wanted to write to you and let you know about a thing or two that's happened here in Fairweather since you left. As you can probably tell from the penmanship, I am not writing this myself as my wrist is still in a cast. Instead, I asked your soon-to-be Aunt Bonnie to take this down and make sure it gets mailed to you. That's right; she's agreed to marry me, but not for another year. Here's the deal:

Thanks to the accident, the draft board has re-classified me 4-F, meaning unfit for military service. As a result, I'm not going into the Marines, not going to Vietnam, and not learning

aircraft mechanics from the Corps. But it turns
out there's a trade school down in Tulsa that offers
the same training, so I'll still be able to work on
jets after I'm better. The catch is, I've got to have a
high school diploma in order to get in, so you can
see how this all sort of falls into place. Plus,
during the time I was in the hospital (nearly three
weeks thanks to the surgery), I had to quit
smoking, so it looks like the score is Bonnie 3,
Bob zero. (Ouch! She just poked me with her pencil
on my good arm.)

There's another thing. About two weeks ago, Lee
Lathrop walked into the Sheriff's Office and
announced that he had information about who
killed Lewis Tate. Well, they listened to his story
and then the night before last they arrested three
old boys here in Fairweather and charged them
with murder. I guess one of them was friends with
Lee and got to bragging about how they had done
it and Lee decided he couldn't just let it go. He

said he wanted to do the right thing. Said it was something you told him. Word is, he might have to lay low for a while in order to preserve his own skin, but I'm not so sure. I have a feeling this will all blow over pretty soon and then things will be back to normal. Well, maybe not quite. Some rich family on the north side of town felt bad about what happened, so they offered Lewis's wife a housekeeping job that comes with live-in privileges. That means his girls will be able to go to the school he wanted them to go to in the first place. I expect that will cause a fuss all around.

Bonnie's giving me a look like she's getting tired so, I got to wrap this up for now, but I wanted to tell you that the night Mom and Dad left for the funeral your friend Gideon came by the hospital to see how I was doing. I wasn't supposed to be having any visitors, so I don't know how he got in here, but he did. I wasn't able to talk to him none, I was still pretty dopey from the surgery and all, but he said he just wanted to find out if I was okay. He didn't stay more than a minute or two, and he hasn't been back since, but dang if he didn't look just like your dad when he was about my age.

Well, that's about all I got to tell you right now, so I'll leave it at so long for a while and I hope you'll be coming down for the wedding next summer. Write back if you get a chance and let me know how you're making out with that Wendy and whether you made the golf team at school.

Your favorite uncle,
Bob

P.S.: Darby got a full scholarship to play golf at Oklahoma State.